Doctor Who

Doctor Who

Matthew Petchinsky

Doctor Who: The TARDIS Confiscation
By: Matthew Petchinsky

Disclaimer:

This is a **fan-made work** inspired by *Doctor Who* and *Men in Black*. It is not affiliated with, endorsed by, or connected to the BBC, Sony Pictures, Marvel Entertainment, or any official license holders of *Doctor Who*, *Men in Black*, or related properties. All characters, organizations, and concepts are used in a transformative, non-commercial, and creative context under fair use. This book is created for entertainment purposes only—by fans, for fans.

Chapter 1: The Unexpected Arrival

The unmistakable groaning wheeze of the TARDIS echoed through an alleyway in New York City, 1997. Its form solidified as a battered blue police box tucked between the graffiti-stained brick walls of two abandoned buildings. A faint mist swirled around the base as the Doctor, with his usual flair, threw open the door and stepped into the crisp autumn air. His long coat flared dramatically as he looked around with wide, curious eyes, already calculating the source of the peculiar energy readings that had brought him here.

"New York City," he muttered, pulling out his sonic screwdriver and scanning the area. "But not just *any* New York. 1997—ah, the year of *Titanic* mania and dial-up modems. Brilliant!" He sniffed the air and smiled. "Smells of hotdogs, impending corporate greed, and—" he paused, his expression turning serious— "a disturbance in the temporal field."

The TARDIS had landed mere blocks from Times Square, its neon lights and billboards blazing in the distance. But something felt off. There was an almost imperceptible hum in the atmosphere, a discordant frequency that made his skin tingle. The Doctor had just begun to adjust the settings on his screwdriver when the sound of approaching footsteps caught his attention.

Two men in black suits emerged from the shadows, their polished shoes clicking against the pavement. They were the epitome of government chic: identical dark sunglasses, earpieces coiled discreetly, and expressions as blank as a freshly wiped whiteboard. One of them carried a sleek, rectangular device that emitted a faint blue glow.

The Doctor raised an eyebrow. "Well, well. Haven't seen this sort of fashion-forward duo since the Galactic Council of 3047. Let me guess: undercover opera singers? Time-traveling barbers? Or perhaps... you're with the local paranormal book club?"

The taller of the two men stepped forward, his voice as flat and monotone as his demeanor. "Sir, you are in possession of an unauthorized temporal displacement device. You are required to hand it over immediately."

The Doctor tilted his head, his grin widening. "Unauthorized? That's a funny word, isn't it? Who exactly is issuing the authorizations these days? Because I must have missed the memo."

The second man, shorter but equally imposing, reached into his jacket and retrieved a small metallic disc. He pressed a button, and a holographic badge flickered into existence, displaying an insignia that looked vaguely familiar to the Doctor.

"Temporal Anomalies Division," the man said. "We monitor and regulate time-travel activity. Your presence here is a breach of protocol."

The Doctor's face lit up with intrigue. "Temporal Anomalies Division! Oh, you're *those* people. I've read about you—well, more like I've skimmed. You lot popped up after the Zygorax Crisis, didn't you? Or was it after the Time Agency got a bit too trigger-happy? Either way, lovely to meet you!"

He extended his hand cheerfully, but neither man took it.

"Doctor," the first man said, his tone sharper now. "We won't ask again. Hand over the device."

The Doctor stepped back, his hands slipping into his coat pockets as he sized them up. "Now, I'd love to stay and chat, maybe exchange stories over a cup of tea, but you see, there's this rather interesting spike in chronon emissions nearby, and I was just about to—"

The shorter man raised the glowing device in his hand, and a burst of energy shot toward the TARDIS. The blue box shuddered, its light dimming momentarily.

"Oi!" the Doctor exclaimed, spinning around to shield the TARDIS with his body. "You don't just shoot someone's time machine! That's rude!"

The taller man adjusted his sunglasses. "Cooperate, or the next shot will disable it permanently."

The Doctor's jovial expression shifted into something far more serious. His eyes darkened, and he straightened to his full height.

"Listen," he said, his voice low and commanding. "You have no idea who you're dealing with. That 'unauthorized device' you're so keen to confiscate? It's not just a machine. It's alive. And if you've damaged her..." He trailed off, letting the threat linger in the air.

The men exchanged a brief glance, their expressions unreadable behind their glasses.

"We know exactly who you are, Doctor," the taller one said. "And if you're here, it means something's gone wrong. You don't just visit 1997 on a whim."

The Doctor narrowed his eyes. "You've been watching me."

"Monitoring," the man corrected. "We're here to ensure that your interference doesn't disrupt the timeline. And right now, you're a risk."

The Doctor stepped closer, his voice dropping to a conspiratorial whisper. "If you think I'm the biggest risk here, you're more clueless than you look. Something's brewing in this city—something big. And I intend to stop it."

The shorter man pressed another button on his device, and a faint ripple passed through the air. The Doctor felt a momentary tug, as if the fabric of reality itself had shifted.

"Temporal lock," the man explained. "You're not going anywhere until we've resolved this."

The Doctor smirked, pulling out his sonic screwdriver. "Ah, love a good challenge. But you really shouldn't try to out-tech the Time Lord." He flicked the sonic, and the ripple dissolved with a sharp buzz.

The two men stared in disbelief as the Doctor brushed past them, heading toward the bustling streets beyond the alley.

"Now, if you'll excuse me," he called over his shoulder, "I've got a mystery to solve. Feel free to tag along, but try not to get in my way. Things tend to get... messy."

The men hesitated for a moment before following, their rigid professionalism masking the unease creeping into their movements.

As the Doctor stepped into the chaos of Times Square, he couldn't help but grin. He could feel it—the crackling energy of an adventure unfolding. And if there was one thing he knew, it was that nothing was ever truly "unexpected" when it came to time.

Chapter 2: MIB Headquarters

The Doctor walked briskly between the two Men in Black, his coat flaring behind him as the three wove through the crowded streets of New York. Despite the unassuming exterior of the Men in Black, he could feel the tension radiating from them—like tightly wound springs ready to snap.

"So," the Doctor began, his tone light but probing, "you two have names, or is this going to be one of those mysterious, clandestine organizations where everyone's just called Agent X, Agent Y, or... I don't know, Agent Zed?"

The taller man, who had introduced himself earlier as Agent K, kept his eyes straight ahead. "You can call me K. This is J. That's all you need to know."

The shorter man, Agent J, turned to the Doctor with a grin that didn't quite hide his curiosity. "And you? You don't have a name either? What's with the whole 'Doctor' thing? You're not, like, a dentist, are you?"

The Doctor smirked. "No, but I have pulled a few teeth in my time—Daleks, mostly. And once, this very nasty Sycorax leader with a terrible sense of dental hygiene."

J blinked. "Yeah, I'm gonna pretend I understood any of that."

The trio reached a nondescript pawn shop with a flickering neon sign that read "Joe's Antiques." K held the door open, and the Doctor stepped inside, his brow arching as he took in the eclectic collection of dusty trinkets, vintage radios, and mismatched furniture.

"Really?" the Doctor quipped. "A pawn shop? Bit on the nose, don't you think?"

K didn't answer, instead nodding to the shopkeeper, a wiry old man with a pair of thick glasses perched on his nose. The man pressed a hidden button under the counter, and with a soft *whirr*, a section of the floor slid away, revealing a sleek metal elevator.

"Ah," the Doctor said, stepping into the elevator with the Agents. "Classic secret entrance. Points for style."

The elevator descended rapidly, the hum of advanced machinery filling the enclosed space. As the doors opened, the Doctor found himself staring at a sprawling underground facility brimming with activity.

Aliens of every conceivable shape and size moved about, some walking on two legs, others slithering or floating. Monitors displayed feeds of space traffic, and technicians worked at sleek consoles, their fingers flying over glowing holographic keyboards.

The Doctor stepped out, his eyes wide with fascination. "Oh, this is *brilliant*! Look at all these species—some of them I haven't seen in centuries! Is that a Boglodite? And over there—oh, a Zarthian Swiveler! You've got quite the collection here."

J raised an eyebrow. "You know these guys?"

"Know them?" The Doctor grinned. "I've probably crashed at least three weddings in this room alone. Lovely people, the Zarthians. Terrible dancers, though."

K cleared his throat. "Enough sightseeing. Follow me."

The Agents led the Doctor down a corridor lined with containment cells, some holding small, fidgeting creatures, others housing ominous, shadowy figures that watched silently as they passed.

They entered a large conference room dominated by a round table. At its center was a glowing holographic projection of Earth, surrounded by orbiting dots that represented various alien crafts.

Seated at the table was a stern-looking man in a crisp black suit, his silver hair and piercing eyes giving him an air of authority.

"Agent Zed," K said, gesturing to the man. "This is the Doctor."

Zed regarded the Doctor with a mixture of suspicion and curiosity. "So, this is the unauthorized time traveler."

The Doctor offered a cheeky grin. "Oh, don't worry. I authorized myself. Saves on paperwork."

Zed wasn't amused. "You're in possession of an alien device—your so-called TARDIS—that has been flagged as a potential security risk. Care to explain?"

The Doctor leaned back, hands in his coat pockets. "The TARDIS isn't just an alien device—it's a Time Lord ship, the last of its kind. She's not a risk to Earth; she's saved it more times than I can count. And before you ask, no, you can't have her."

Zed's expression hardened. "This facility's purpose is to protect Earth from extraterrestrial threats. Anything we can't control is a threat."

"Control?" The Doctor's tone sharpened. "You don't control the TARDIS. She's not a machine; she's alive. And trust me, you don't want to get on her bad side."

J, who had been leaning against the wall, interjected. "Hold up. Alive? Like, she's got feelings and stuff?"

The Doctor nodded. "Oh, yes. And she's very protective of me."

Zed wasn't convinced. "Regardless, the TARDIS will be secured in our containment bay until further notice."

The Doctor stepped forward, his voice taking on a commanding edge. "You're making a mistake. Whatever's causing those energy readings—it's dangerous. I can help you stop it, but I need the TARDIS."

K crossed his arms. "And why should we trust you?"

The Doctor locked eyes with him. "Because while you're busy cataloging threats, I've been out there fighting them. I've seen things that would turn your hair gray—well, grayer."

J stifled a chuckle, earning a glare from K.

Zed studied the Doctor for a long moment before speaking. "You've got one chance. Prove that you're here to help, or the TARDIS stays locked up, and you'll be our next containment project."

The Doctor smiled, clapping his hands together. "Excellent! Now, let's get to work. Where do you keep your anomalous energy reports? Or should I just guess?"

J gestured to a nearby console. "Knock yourself out, Doc. But if you try anything funny..." He tapped his neuralyzer with a smirk.

The Doctor raised a brow. "Oh, please. That flashy little gadget? Amateur hour. But nice try."

As the Doctor began poring over the data, a low rumble reverberated through the facility. The lights flickered, and a warning alarm blared.

Zed's voice cut through the noise. "What the hell is that?"

The Doctor straightened, his face grim. "That," he said, pointing to the holographic projection, which now displayed a rapidly growing red dot near the city, "is what I came to stop."

And with that, the Doctor dashed toward the door, leaving the Agents scrambling to keep up. "Come on, then! Adventure awaits!" he called over his shoulder.

Chapter 3: The Confiscation

The TARDIS sat at the center of a gleaming containment bay, surrounded by towering metal walls and an array of complex security systems. Men in black suits moved with precision, setting up scanning equipment and holographic projectors. The Doctor stood outside the transparent containment barrier, his hands stuffed deep into his coat pockets, his face a mask of restrained irritation.

"This is completely unnecessary," the Doctor declared, his voice echoing in the cavernous space. "The TARDIS isn't dangerous, and if she's offended, she might just leave on her own. You don't want to see her when she's sulking."

Agent K, standing a few paces away, didn't flinch. "Protocol is protocol. Any alien technology entering Earth's atmosphere has to be examined and, if necessary, neutralized. Your... TARDIS is no exception."

The Doctor turned to him, his tone dripping with sarcasm. "Oh, splendid. Let's neutralize the one thing standing between this planet and a hundred different apocalypses. Brilliant strategy, that."

Agent J stepped in, trying to defuse the tension. "Hey, Doc, look, I get it. She's your ride, your pride and joy. But we've got rules here. And rules? They keep this rock spinning without a million aliens setting up shop."

The Doctor spun around, his coat flaring dramatically. "Do you even hear yourselves? The TARDIS is *not* just a 'ride.' She's a living, breathing—well, metaphorically—piece of advanced Time Lord engineering! She's beyond anything your little scanners can comprehend." He gestured toward the containment chamber. "And now you're poking her with your primitive gadgets like toddlers trying to figure out a Rubik's Cube."

J muttered under his breath, "Man, this guy's extra."

Zed entered the room, his expression stony. "Doctor, your cooperation is appreciated, but it's not required. The TARDIS is now classified as a Class-X threat until we understand its capabilities. If you attempt to interfere, you will be detained permanently."

The Doctor's expression darkened, and for a moment, his usual joviality gave way to something far more intense. He stepped closer to Zed, his voice low and dangerous. "Do you have any idea what you're dealing with? The TARDIS has been through wars, survived black holes, and traveled to the beginning and end of time. She's saved this universe more times than you can count. And now you're locking her up like some trinket you found in a flea market?"

Zed didn't flinch. "This isn't up for debate. You're under our jurisdiction now."

"Jurisdiction?" the Doctor scoffed, throwing his hands in the air. "I was here before your *jurisdiction* was even a twinkle in humanity's eye! I've faced creatures that would devour this planet in seconds, and you're worried about a blue box?"

J tried to interject, but K raised a hand, his gaze fixed on the Doctor. "You're not helping your case. If the TARDIS is as important as you say, then prove it by working with us instead of against us."

The Doctor took a deep breath, visibly reigning in his temper. He looked at the TARDIS, her windows dim and her light eerily still.

"Fine," he said finally, his voice quiet but firm. "But if she so much as hiccups in protest, it's on your heads. And I do mean that literally—she can get quite creative when she's upset."

As the Doctor stepped back, the containment barrier sealed with a low hum. He turned to leave but paused at the door, glancing over his shoulder.

"Be careful," he warned, his tone soft but laced with steel. "You're playing with forces you can't begin to understand."

In the main observation room, the Doctor was reluctantly escorted to a desk filled with MIB's most advanced technology. Screens displayed real-time readouts of the TARDIS's interior—though the data was an incomprehensible mess of shifting symbols and error codes.

"Well," the Doctor said, leaning over to peer at the screens. "At least your tech is trying. Points for effort, I suppose."

J leaned against the wall, watching him with a mix of amusement and curiosity. "So, what's the deal with you and that box? You two married or something?"

The Doctor rolled his eyes. "Not married. Partners. She takes me where I'm needed—sometimes where I don't want to go but need to be. It's a symbiotic relationship. She's more than a ship; she's... home."

K, standing nearby, crossed his arms. "If she's so advanced, why bring her here? Why not stay out there?" He gestured upward.

The Doctor straightened, his expression unreadable. "Because out there doesn't matter if down here is destroyed. Earth has a habit of attracting trouble—big, nasty, universe-ending trouble. And someone has to stop it."

J smirked. "So, you're like a galactic janitor? Clean up the mess, move on to the next one?"

"Something like that," the Doctor replied with a faint smile. "Though I prefer 'heroic wanderer.'"

As they spoke, the room's alarms suddenly blared. A technician at a nearby console called out, "We're detecting a surge in temporal energy! It's coming from the containment bay!"

The Doctor's head snapped up, and he bolted for the door. "I told you!" he shouted over his shoulder.

K and J exchanged a look before following.

Back in the containment bay, the TARDIS was glowing faintly, her light pulsing like a heartbeat. The containment field flickered as the readings on the monitors spiraled into chaos.

"What did you do to her?" the Doctor demanded, rushing into the room.

Zed appeared on a nearby platform, barking orders. "Shut it down! Stabilize the field!"

"Don't!" the Doctor shouted. "She's reacting to your interference. You're only making it worse!"

The technicians hesitated, unsure whether to follow Zed's orders or heed the Doctor's warning.

K placed a hand on Zed's arm. "Let him handle it. If he's right, we can't afford to risk it."

Reluctantly, Zed nodded, and the Doctor approached the TARDIS. He placed a hand on her door, his expression softening.

"Easy, old girl," he murmured. "It's me. I'm here."

The light steadied, and the containment field stabilized. The Doctor turned to face the stunned MIB agents.

"She doesn't like being caged," he said simply. "Neither do I. Now, are you going to listen to me, or are we going to keep playing this ridiculous game?"

Zed stared at him for a long moment before responding. "You've got our attention. But one wrong move, and the TARDIS goes back into lockdown."

The Doctor nodded, a small smile tugging at the corners of his mouth. "Good. Now, let's figure out what's really going on, shall we?"

Chapter 4: The Bug Problem

The Doctor paced the sleek, metallic observation deck at MIB headquarters, his mind buzzing with possibilities. The TARDIS sat in containment, quiet for now, but his growing frustration at being separated from her was palpable. Nearby, Agent J leaned against a console, idly flipping through alien profiles on a tablet, while Agent K studied a holographic map of New York City.

The room's intercom crackled, and a sharp, panicked voice cut through the low hum of machinery. "Agent K, we've got a situation. Level five alert. There's a Class-3 alien disturbance downtown—coordinates are incoming."

K stiffened, his face unreadable, as the holographic map updated to show a red pulsating dot in Midtown Manhattan. "What kind of disturbance?"

The voice hesitated. "Uh... it's a Bug. A big one. Reports say it's tearing through buildings and scaring the locals. Witnesses claim it's looking for something, but we don't know what."

"A Bug?" The Doctor perked up, his eyes gleaming with curiosity. "Oh, I love Bugs. Big, nasty, terrible table manners, but they always make for an interesting day. What species are we talking? Skaraxian Beetle? Zygorian Hive Mother? Or—"

"It's not a picnic, Doc," J interrupted. "If it's a Bug, it's bad news. Trust me, they're not here for sightseeing."

K grabbed his neuralyzer and a sleek alien weapon from the armory rack. "Suit up. We're heading out."

The Doctor strode forward, hands clasped behind his back. "You'll need me for this."

K turned, his expression skeptical. "And why's that?"

"Because," the Doctor said, drawing out the word as he leaned against the console, "Bugs don't just show up on Earth without a reason. If it's tearing up Midtown, it's not random. It's hunting for something—or someone—and I can help figure out what."

J snorted. "Yeah, and what's in it for you? Besides, last time I checked, you're not exactly on the guest list."

The Doctor smiled, unbothered. "Oh, I never work for selfish reasons, Agent J. I simply hate seeing a good planet ruined by bad intentions. Besides..." He pointed at the map. "I've dealt with creatures like this before. Do you want my help or not?"

K considered for a moment, his eyes narrowing as he sized up the Doctor. Finally, he nodded. "Fine. But you follow our lead. One wrong move, and you're back in containment with your box."

"Deal," the Doctor said, already striding toward the exit.

Midtown Manhattan

The scene was chaos. Sirens wailed as emergency vehicles cordoned off streets. Civilians scattered in all directions, screaming as a massive, chitinous creature rampaged through a row of storefronts. The Bug stood over twenty feet tall, its segmented body glistening in the afternoon sun. Jagged mandibles snapped menacingly, and its multifaceted eyes scanned its surroundings with unsettling focus.

The Doctor, J, and K arrived in a sleek black MIB cruiser that glided to a stop a safe distance from the chaos.

"Well," the Doctor said, stepping out and adjusting his coat. "She's a beauty, isn't she? Look at those mandibles—perfect for crushing bones. And the exoskeleton? Marvelously reflective. Textbook predatory design."

J glanced at him, incredulous. "You're admiring it? That thing's about to turn this block into a Bug buffet!"

"Ah, but that's the thing," the Doctor replied, his sonic screwdriver already in hand. "Bugs like this don't expend energy without a purpose. She's looking for something."

K was already scanning the area with his own device. "What exactly do you think she's after, Doc?"

The Doctor pointed at the Bug's erratic movements. It smashed a car with one swipe of its clawed limb but didn't linger, instead continuing to sift through debris, lifting and discarding rubble with alarming speed.

"She's searching for something small," the Doctor deduced. "Maybe an egg, a larva, or—" He paused, his face lighting up with understanding. "—a tracker."

"Tracker?" J repeated.

The Doctor nodded. "Someone's hunting her, and she knows it. She's not just destructive; she's desperate."

Before the Agents could respond, the Bug turned toward their group, its mandibles clicking ominously.

"Uh, Doc," J said, stepping back, "you might wanna rethink the whole admiration thing, 'cause it looks like we're next on the menu."

The Doctor raised his hands in mock surrender. "Now, now, let's not be hasty." He turned to the Bug and shouted, "Hello there! I'm the Doctor! Fancy a chat?"

The Bug screeched, a piercing sound that rattled nearby windows. It charged toward them with alarming speed.

"Not much for conversation, are you?" the Doctor muttered, dodging behind a parked car as K and J opened fire with their weapons.

Blasts of green energy struck the Bug's armored body, but the creature barely flinched. It lashed out, its claws narrowly missing J, who dove out of the way with a yell.

"This isn't working!" K shouted.

The Doctor peeked out from his hiding spot, his mind racing. Then he spotted something glinting on the Bug's underbelly—a small, circular device embedded in its exoskeleton.

"There!" he called, pointing. "That's the tracker! We need to remove it!"

J stared at him like he'd grown a second head. "You wanna get close enough to that thing to play doctor? Are you nuts?"

"Well, I am *the* Doctor," he quipped, darting out into the open.

"Doc!" J yelled, but the Time Lord was already sprinting toward the Bug.

The creature turned, its mandibles snapping, but the Doctor was quicker. He slid beneath its massive body, narrowly avoiding a crushing limb, and activated his sonic screwdriver. The tracker sparked and sizzled as the sonic emitted a high-pitched whine.

The Bug froze, emitting a low, guttural growl.

"Almost... got it..." the Doctor muttered, twisting the screwdriver's settings. With a final burst of energy, the tracker popped free, and the Bug reeled back, its movements less frantic.

The Doctor scrambled out from under it, holding up the device triumphantly. "There! Now, let's see who's been bugging our friend here."

The tracker emitted a faint signal, which the Doctor quickly linked to K's scanner. A map of New York appeared, a new red dot blinking several blocks away.

"Someone's controlling it," the Doctor said. "And I think we've just found our culprit."

The Bug, now calmer, gave the group a final screech before scuttling off into the shadows.

"Well," J said, staring after it, "that's not how I thought this would go."

The Doctor dusted off his coat. "Stick with me, J. Things rarely go as expected. Now, let's pay a visit to whoever's pulling the strings, shall we?"

K nodded grimly. "Agreed. But this time, Doctor, you follow *our* lead."

The Doctor grinned. "Of course, Agent K. Whatever you say."

But his eyes sparkled with excitement. The mystery was only just beginning.

Chapter 5: A Reluctant Partnership

Back at MIB headquarters, the atmosphere was tense. The holographic map in the central command room displayed the Bug's last known trajectory, a pulsing red dot moving erratically across the screen. Agents bustled around, their faces grim as they prepared for the next phase of the operation.

The Doctor leaned casually against a console, spinning the recovered tracker between his fingers. His expression was calm, almost amused, which only seemed to irritate Agent K further.

"This isn't a game," K said, his tone clipped. "That thing is still out there, and it's not gonna stop until it finds what it's looking for—or we stop it."

"Agreed," the Doctor said brightly, tossing the tracker into the air and catching it. "Which is why you'll need me. Bugs aren't just mindless brutes, you know. They're surprisingly clever—strategic, even. Whoever planted this tracker knew that. And now..." He pointed dramatically to the map. "They're using the chaos to cover their tracks."

K folded his arms, unimpressed. "We've handled worse without your help."

"Yeah, but not like this," Agent J interjected, stepping between them. "Look, K, I know you don't trust him—I don't fully trust him either—but you gotta admit, the guy knows his alien stuff. I mean, he got that tracker off the Bug without becoming Bug chow. That's gotta count for something."

K's eyes narrowed as he regarded the Doctor. "What's your angle in all this? You could've walked away, let us deal with it. Why stick around?"

The Doctor's grin faded slightly, replaced by a more serious expression. "Because I don't like seeing creatures used as pawns in someone else's game. That Bug isn't the real threat. It's scared, confused, and trying to survive. Whoever planted this tracker—they're the ones pulling the strings. And if we don't stop them, more people will get hurt."

J nodded. "See? That's what I'm saying. The Doc's got a point."

K sighed, pinching the bridge of his nose. "Alright, fine. You're in. But you follow our protocols. No going rogue, no running off on your own, and no more of that... improvisation you seem so fond of."

The Doctor beamed. "Oh, improvisation is my middle name! Well, actually, it's more of a philosophy, but—"

"Doctor," K interrupted, his tone warning.

"Right, yes, follow the rules. Got it." The Doctor clapped his hands together. "So, where do we start?"

The Bug's Trail

The trio piled into an MIB cruiser, its sleek, black exterior blending seamlessly with the night. Inside, the dashboard flickered with alien technology, and a holographic projection of the city hovered above the center console.

J piloted the vehicle, his hands steady on the wheel as the cruiser sped through the streets in near silence. The Doctor sat in the back, his sonic screwdriver scanning the tracker he had removed from the Bug.

"This is fascinating," the Doctor said, holding the tracker up to the light. "It's not just a simple locator—it's a bio-interface. Whoever designed this wanted to control the Bug's actions, not just monitor its movements."

"Control it?" J asked, glancing at the Doctor through the rearview mirror.

"Exactly," the Doctor replied, his tone growing more serious. "Bugs of this size and intelligence aren't easy to manipulate. They're fiercely independent. But this tracker is emitting a frequency that disrupts their natural instincts—overrides them, even. It's cruel, really."

K, seated in the passenger seat, frowned. "Any idea who's behind it?"

"Not yet," the Doctor admitted, his brow furrowing. "But the signal is being relayed from a central hub. If we trace it, we'll find the puppeteer."

The cruiser's onboard system chimed, and a new blip appeared on the map—a glowing green dot intersecting the Bug's trail.

"Got something," J said, tapping the display. "That's the last known location of the signal's origin."

"Then let's not keep them waiting," the Doctor said, leaning forward with a mischievous grin.

The Abandoned Warehouse

The cruiser came to a stop outside a decrepit warehouse on the outskirts of the city. The building loomed in the darkness, its windows shattered and its walls covered in graffiti.

"This place screams bad guy lair," J muttered, stepping out of the vehicle.

"Classic," the Doctor agreed, adjusting his coat as he followed. "Abandoned warehouses, secret labs, underground bunkers—villains do love their clichés."

K led the way, his weapon drawn. "Stay alert. Whoever's in there, they've got the tech to control a Bug. That makes them dangerous."

The trio entered cautiously, their footsteps echoing on the concrete floor. Inside, the air was thick with the hum of machinery. Banks of monitors lined one wall, displaying live feeds of the Bug's rampage. At the center of the room was a makeshift control station, manned by a wiry figure in a lab coat.

The man turned at their approach, his face pale and gaunt. His eyes widened when he saw them. "Who—how did you find this place?"

"Easy," the Doctor said, stepping forward. "Follow the Bug, find the villain. Really, you didn't make it that hard."

The man sneered. "You don't understand. That creature is mine—it's a masterpiece of genetic engineering!"

The Doctor's expression darkened. "It's a living being, not a science experiment. And you've tortured it for your own gain."

K leveled his weapon at the man. "Step away from the controls. Now."

The scientist hesitated, his hand hovering over a console. "You think you can stop me? The Bug is just the beginning. With my technology, I can control any alien species—turn them into the perfect weapons!"

"Not if I have anything to say about it," the Doctor said, raising his sonic screwdriver.

The scientist lunged for the console, but before he could activate it, K fired a precision shot that disabled the controls. Sparks flew, and the machinery sputtered to a halt.

"No!" the man shouted, scrambling to salvage his work.

The Doctor stepped forward, his voice calm but firm. "It's over. You've lost."

The scientist glared at him, seething. "You don't understand what you're meddling with! The Bug—it's already bonded to the signal. If you destroy the tracker, it'll go berserk!"

The Doctor's eyes narrowed. "Then we'd better find a way to calm her down. And you're going to help us."

As the Agents restrained the scientist, the Doctor turned to the monitors, his mind racing.

"We need to get back to the Bug," he said. "She's still out there, and if we don't act fast, she'll tear the city apart."

J nodded, already moving toward the exit. "Then let's roll. The sooner we deal with this, the better."

K followed, his expression grim. "This partnership better be worth it, Doctor."

The Doctor grinned, his determination shining through. "Oh, it will be. Trust me."

And with that, the chase was on.

Chapter 6: Tracing the Bug

The Doctor, Agent J, and Agent K stood in the MIB operations room, where a massive holographic map of New York City floated above the center console. The red dot representing the Bug's location pulsed intermittently, indicating its movements through the city. MIB technicians worked tirelessly at their consoles, filtering through reports of destruction, eyewitness accounts, and alien activity.

Agent K leaned against the console, arms crossed, his face impassive. "The Bug's trail is erratic. She's not staying in one place long enough for us to pin her down."

The Doctor stood nearby, sonic screwdriver in hand, tapping it rhythmically against his palm as he stared at the map. "No, no, no, K, you're thinking too linearly. Bugs don't think like humans—they're goal-oriented, single-minded. She's not just causing chaos for the fun of it. She's looking for something."

J, seated at the console, frowned as he scanned through the reports. "Yeah, well, she's looking with claws and mandibles. Just got word she smashed through a penthouse uptown. Fancy place, owned by some big-shot real estate mogul—or, well, 'mogul' on paper. Turns out he's an alien."

The Doctor perked up at that. "An alien, you say? What species?"

J shrugged. "Something called a... um..." He squinted at the screen. "Galvantian. Says here they're big into tech and trade, low-profile, no known hostile tendencies."

The Doctor's face lit up. "Oh, Galvantians! Brilliant engineers. Bit overly paranoid, but that's understandable when you're sitting on tech that half the galaxy would kill to get their hands on." He turned to K. "If the Bug targeted a Galvantian, then she wasn't after a snack. She's after something specific."

K straightened. "What kind of something?"

"Let's find out," the Doctor said, already heading for the exit. "To the penthouse!"

The Penthouse

The trio arrived at the destroyed penthouse in record time, their MIB cruiser gliding to a stop in front of the gleaming skyscraper. A large section of the building's top floor had been torn apart, with glass and debris littering the street below. Police had cordoned off the area, but MIB agents were already on-site, their black suits a stark contrast to the chaos.

Inside the penthouse, the destruction was even more apparent. Expensive furniture lay in ruins, walls were clawed open, and a shimmering silver device in the corner emitted a low hum. The Doctor crouched near a shattered table, examining the claw marks with his sonic screwdriver.

"Look at these scratches," he murmured. "Precise, deliberate. She wasn't rampaging—she was searching." He pointed to a torn-up section of the wall. "See there? She was trying to get at whatever was behind that panel."

Agent J knelt beside him, his brow furrowed. "You're telling me she knew exactly where to look? Bugs aren't exactly known for their detective skills."

"Not on their own," the Doctor agreed, standing and pacing the room. "But with that tracker's influence? It could enhance her instincts, guiding her to a target."

K joined them, gesturing toward the silver device. "That's a Galvantian safe. High-tech, nearly indestructible. Whatever was in there is gone."

The Doctor turned sharply. "Gone? Someone got to it first?"

"No," said a shaky voice from the corner. The group turned to see a disheveled man—tall, with slightly luminescent eyes and faint ridges along his forehead. He was sitting amidst the debris, clutching a large blanket around himself. "The Bug... she took it."

"And you are?" the Doctor asked, kneeling down to meet the man's gaze.

"My name is Varnix," the man replied, his voice trembling. "I'm the owner of this penthouse—or was." He gestured weakly at the ruins around him. "The Bug came for my star shard."

"Star shard?" J repeated, looking at the Doctor for clarification.

The Doctor's eyes widened. "A star shard? Oh, that's very bad. Very, very bad. Varnix, why do you have a star shard on Earth? They're dangerously unstable, not to mention highly sought after by less-than-scrupulous beings."

Varnix swallowed hard. "It's an ancient relic from my people. I brought it here for safekeeping, but... someone must have found out."

K narrowed his eyes. "What exactly does this star shard do?"

The Doctor stood, his expression grave. "It's not just a shiny rock. Star shards are fragments of a collapsed star, capable of storing immense amounts of energy. In the wrong hands, they could be used as a weapon—a very destructive one."

Varnix nodded. "The Bug must have been sent to retrieve it. But for whom? And why?"

The Doctor turned to the agents, his mind racing. "This changes everything. The Bug isn't acting on instinct—it's being used. Someone planted that tracker and is using her to collect the shard. If they succeed in weaponizing it—"

J cut in, his tone sharp. "Then we're all toast."

"Precisely," the Doctor said. He pulled out his sonic screwdriver and began scanning the room. "We need to trace the Bug's next move. If the shard is what she was after, she's likely headed to a rendezvous point to deliver it to whoever's controlling her."

K pulled out his communicator, barking orders. "Get me a city-wide sweep for anomalous energy signatures. Focus on locations that could serve as a meeting point. I want answers now."

The Doctor glanced at K, impressed. "Efficient. I like that."

J crossed his arms, his expression grim. "Alright, Doc. You said this star shard is dangerous. How dangerous are we talking?"

The Doctor's expression darkened. "Think planet-shattering. In the wrong hands, it could wipe out entire civilizations. And whoever's behind this knows that."

A New Lead

Moments later, a technician's voice came through K's earpiece. "Agent K, we've got a hit. An energy spike consistent with the shard's properties just appeared near the East River. It's faint but steady."

"That's our rendezvous point," K said. He turned to the Doctor and J. "Let's move."

The Doctor nodded, his usual grin replaced by a look of determination. "Time to save the day, then. And let's hope we're not too late."

As they headed out, the Doctor couldn't shake the feeling that the true mastermind behind the Bug was watching their every move. The game was far from over.

Chapter 7: The Escape

The MIB cruiser sped toward the East River, its engines humming with a barely perceptible alien frequency. Inside, Agent J gripped the steering controls tightly, his knuckles white, while K sat beside him, his face set in grim determination. In the back seat, the Doctor adjusted his bow tie—always a fan of dressing for the occasion—while glancing over his sonic screwdriver, its faint whir a comforting sound in the tense silence.

"You've faced Bugs like this before, right?" J asked, breaking the quiet.

"Oh, plenty," the Doctor replied casually, leaning back. "Big ones, small ones, ones that spit acid, ones that—"

"Spare us the list, Doc," K interjected. "What's the plan when we get there?"

"Plan?" The Doctor looked up, his face bright with curiosity. "Oh, no plan. Plans are boring. We improvise."

J groaned. "Man, you really need to stop saying that."

The Doctor grinned. "Why? It works—most of the time."

The East River Dockyard

The cruiser came to a halt near an abandoned dockyard, its skeletal cranes looming against the night sky. The air smelled of salt and rust, and the distant sound of water lapping against the pier filled the quiet. The area was eerily deserted, save for the faint glint of movement among the shadows.

"There," K said, pointing toward a warehouse with a partially collapsed roof. "That's where the energy spike is coming from."

The Doctor scanned the building with his screwdriver. "Ah, yes. Lots of temporal energy swirling about. And...oh!" He froze mid-scan, his expression darkening. "She's here."

"How do you know?" J whispered, his weapon drawn.

The Doctor gestured toward the faint claw marks etched into the ground leading to the warehouse. "Because Bugs are messy eaters, but meticulous hunters."

As they crept closer, a low, guttural screech echoed from inside the warehouse, followed by the unmistakable sound of metal crunching.

"Yup," J muttered. "Definitely here."

Inside the Warehouse

The interior was a scene of destruction. Stacks of rusted shipping containers lay toppled, their contents scattered across the concrete floor. In the center of the chaos stood the Bug, its massive form illuminated by the flickering glow of an alien device that pulsed with unnatural light. Clutched in its claws was the star shard, its surface shimmering with an ethereal glow.

"That's it," the Doctor whispered. "The shard."

Before anyone could respond, the Bug turned its multifaceted eyes toward the group, letting out a deafening screech. The sound reverberated through the warehouse, sending shivers down everyone's spine.

"Time for improvisation," the Doctor said, stepping forward, hands raised. "Hello again! I'm the Doctor. You remember me, don't you? We had a lovely chat earlier—well, I talked, you screeched. Let's not fight, hmm?"

The Bug hissed, its mandibles snapping violently.

"Not much of a conversationalist," J muttered, aiming his weapon.

"Wait!" the Doctor snapped, holding out a hand. "Don't shoot! She's scared."

"Scared?" K said, his voice incredulous. "She's holding a weapon that could destroy the planet."

"Exactly," the Doctor said, his tone softening. "She doesn't want to hurt anyone. She's being forced to do this."

The Bug shifted, its claws tightening around the shard as it let out another screech. The Doctor took a cautious step closer, his sonic screwdriver buzzing softly.

"I know you don't want to do this," he said, his voice calm and steady. "You're just trying to survive. But that thing you're holding—it's dangerous. It could hurt you, too."

The Bug hesitated, its movements slowing. For a moment, it seemed as though the Doctor's words were getting through. But then, a high-pitched tone emitted from the shard, causing the Bug to writhe in agony.

"No!" the Doctor shouted. "Someone's triggering the tracker remotely!"

The Bug turned wild, lashing out at its surroundings. A massive claw swiped toward the group, and they barely dodged in time. K and J fired their weapons, green energy blasts striking the Bug's exoskeleton but doing little more than angering it further.

"That's not helping!" the Doctor yelled over the chaos. "We need to disable the tracker!"

J ducked behind a shipping container. "And how exactly do we do that, genius?"

The Doctor's eyes darted to the shard, then back to his sonic screwdriver. "We overload the tracker's frequency. It'll destabilize the control signal and give her back her free will!"

"And how long will that take?" K demanded, firing another shot to keep the Bug at bay.

"About ten seconds, give or take," the Doctor said, darting toward the Bug.

"Doc, no!" J shouted.

But the Doctor was already moving. He slid under the Bug's massive frame, narrowly avoiding its snapping claws, and pointed his screwdriver at the shard. The device whirred, emitting a high-pitched tone that caused the shard to glow brighter.

The Bug let out an ear-splitting screech and swiped at the Doctor, forcing him to roll out of the way. "Just a little more time!" he muttered.

K and J continued to fire, trying to distract the Bug long enough for the Doctor to complete his task. Finally, with a burst of energy, the shard flickered and went dark.

The Bug froze, its movements suddenly sluggish. It looked around, confused, as though waking from a nightmare. But before anyone could act, it let out a low growl and scuttled toward a nearby wall, crashing through the steel plating and disappearing into the night.

The Aftermath

The warehouse fell silent, save for the sound of debris settling. The Doctor stood, dusting off his coat, and sighed. "Well, that could've gone better."

J stared at the hole in the wall, shaking his head. "Could've gone worse, too. At least she didn't squash us."

K approached the shard, now lying inert on the ground. He picked it up carefully, inspecting its surface. "What's next, Doc?"

The Doctor frowned, crouching to examine a series of symbols etched into the floor near where the shard had been. The symbols glowed faintly, their intricate patterns pulsating with residual energy.

"What's that?" J asked, peering over the Doctor's shoulder.

The Doctor's expression darkened. "A message. Left by whoever's controlling her."

K leaned in, his brow furrowed. "What does it say?"

The Doctor traced the symbols with his finger, his voice low. "It's a warning. 'The shard is only the beginning.'" He stood, his face grim. "This isn't just about the Bug or the shard. This is part of a much larger plot."

J groaned. "Great. So we've got some big bad pulling the strings?"

The Doctor nodded. "And whoever they are, they're just getting started."

K exchanged a look with J, then turned to the Doctor. "Then we'd better stop them before it's too late."

The Doctor's smile returned, but it was tinged with determination. "Oh, you can count on that. Now, let's see where this rabbit hole leads, shall we?"

Chapter 8: TARDIS Secrets

The Doctor paced the MIB command center, his hands shoved deep into his coat pockets, his face a mix of worry and determination. Around him, agents worked frantically at their stations, compiling reports of strange energy fluctuations across the city. The holographic map displayed an alarming pattern: a web of temporal distortions radiating outward, with the TARDIS at the epicenter.

"Doctor," Agent K said, his tone sharp. "If you've got any idea what's going on, now's the time to share."

The Doctor paused mid-stride, turning to face K, his eyes flashing with urgency. "Oh, I have more than an idea. I know exactly what's going on. The Bug isn't just some random predator wreaking havoc. She's been manipulated, controlled, and sent here for a purpose."

Agent J leaned against a nearby console, arms crossed. "Yeah, we got that part. What's she after?"

The Doctor pointed to the map. "The TARDIS."

A stunned silence fell over the room. K's jaw tightened, while J blinked in disbelief. "Your box? Why would she want that?"

The Doctor stepped closer to the holographic display, his voice steady but filled with gravity. "The TARDIS isn't just a time machine; it's a doorway. She can travel through time and space, yes, but her true power lies in her ability to manipulate the fabric of reality itself. To a species like the Bug—or more importantly, to whoever's controlling her—the TARDIS is the ultimate weapon."

K frowned, his eyes narrowing. "Weapon? How?"

"Interdimensional rifts," the Doctor explained, gesturing animatedly. "The TARDIS can create stable passageways between dimensions, universes, timelines. With her, you could open portals large enough to bring through an entire invasion force—or worse, destabilize the barriers between dimensions entirely. It would be catastrophic."

J whistled low. "Okay, so this isn't just about stomping on cars and eating a few unlucky people. This is end-of-the-world stuff."

"End of *everything* stuff," the Doctor corrected, his voice sharp. "And right now, the Bug's controller knows exactly where she is. If we don't stop them, they'll break into the TARDIS and use her to rip reality apart."

K folded his arms. "And what do you propose we do?"

The Doctor turned to him, his expression fierce. "You give her back to me."

J raised an eyebrow. "Just like that? After all the trouble we went through to lock her up?"

"Just like that," the Doctor said, stepping closer to K. "Look, I know you don't trust me. Fair enough. But the TARDIS is more than just my ship. She's alive. She responds to me and only me. If you think your containment protocols will stop someone determined enough to break in, you're wrong. The TARDIS will defend herself, but even she has limits. Let me help, and I can stop this before it's too late."

K didn't respond immediately, his gaze unreadable. Finally, he glanced at J. "What do you think?"

J scratched the back of his neck, clearly torn. "I don't like it, but... the Doc's got a point. If that Bug gets into the TARDIS, we're all screwed."

K sighed heavily, his expression hardening. "Alright, Doctor. You get your ship back. But you'd better have a plan, and you'd better not screw this up."

The Doctor's grin returned, bright and confident. "Oh, K, when have I ever let you down?"

J snorted. "You really want us to answer that?"

The Containment Bay

The TARDIS stood in the center of the containment bay, her blue exterior gleaming under the harsh fluorescent lights. The Doctor approached her slowly, his hand resting on the wooden door as if greeting an old friend.

"Hello, old girl," he murmured. "Sorry about the delay. Let's get you out of here, shall we?"

The containment field hummed as MIB technicians deactivated it. The Doctor pulled out his key, unlocking the door with a satisfying *click*. He stepped inside, the familiar hum of the TARDIS filling the air like music.

J peered inside, his jaw dropping. "Okay, no way. It's—"

"Bigger on the inside," the Doctor finished with a grin. "Yes, yes, they all say that. Come on, no time to dawdle."

K and J exchanged a look before stepping inside. J's head swiveled, taking in the glowing console, the towering columns, and the endless corridors that seemed to stretch into infinity. "This is insane."

"Focus, Agent J," K said, though even his usual stoicism was tinged with awe.

The Doctor darted to the central console, flipping switches and turning knobs. "Right, let's see where our Bug friend is headed next. If she's still linked to the shard's signal, I can use the TARDIS to triangulate her exact location."

K stepped closer, watching the Doctor work. "What's the plan once we find her?"

The Doctor's hands paused briefly on the console, his face thoughtful. "We convince her to stop."

J raised an eyebrow. "Convince her? Doc, she's a twenty-foot-tall killing machine. How exactly do you plan to have a heart-to-heart with that?"

The Doctor turned to him, his expression calm but firm. "Because she's not just a machine. She's a living creature, and living creatures respond to reason—if you know how to talk to them."

K remained skeptical. "And if that doesn't work?"

The Doctor's face darkened. "Then we deal with the real threat—the one controlling her."

The Chase Begins

The TARDIS groaned as it came to life, its engines sending vibrations through the air. The Doctor flipped a final lever, and the central column began to move.

"Got her!" the Doctor exclaimed, pointing to a monitor displaying a glowing red dot. "She's heading for the city center. That's where the dimensional energy is strongest. Whoever's controlling her is setting up the final phase of their plan."

K nodded. "Then we'd better get there fast."

The Doctor's grin returned, and he threw a switch with dramatic flair. "Hold on, gentlemen. This is going to be bumpy!"

The TARDIS lurched, and with a wheezing groan, it dematerialized, leaving behind the empty containment bay.

The Doctor knew the stakes were higher than ever. The Bug was only a pawn, and the true mastermind was waiting for them. But with the TARDIS back in his hands, the Doctor was ready to face whatever came next.

Chapter 9: An Alien Conspiracy

The TARDIS materialized with its characteristic wheezing groan in the middle of an abandoned subway station. Dust and debris coated the tiles, and faint echoes of dripping water filled the air. The holographic map on the TARDIS console displayed a web of energy signatures, each connected to the Bug's movements and the mysterious alien factions supporting its mission.

The Doctor stepped out first, his long coat swishing as he scanned the darkened station with his sonic screwdriver. Agent J and Agent K followed close behind, their weapons drawn and their expressions tense.

"So, what's the deal, Doc?" J asked, glancing around the eerie space. "Why are we stopping here? This doesn't exactly scream 'epic conspiracy.'"

The Doctor raised a finger, silencing him. "Patience, J. This isn't just an abandoned station—it's a hub." He gestured to the walls, where faint, glowing alien symbols had been carved into the tile. "See these? Communication markers. They're a signal to any extraterrestrial visitors that this is a neutral meeting ground."

K frowned, his sharp eyes studying the symbols. "And what are they meeting about?"

"That's what we're here to find out," the Doctor replied, his voice darkening. "But I'd wager it's not a tea party."

The Hidden Chamber

The trio followed the faint glow of the symbols deeper into the station until they reached a rusted maintenance door. The Doctor scanned it with his screwdriver, and the door hissed open, revealing a staircase that descended into darkness.

"Typical," J muttered, peering into the abyss. "Bad guys always pick the creepiest places."

"Shh!" The Doctor silenced him again, his ears pricking up. From below, faint voices echoed—alien voices, speaking in a guttural, rhythmic language.

The group descended cautiously, the Doctor leading the way. At the bottom of the stairs, they entered a cavernous chamber lit by a strange, pulsating green light. A group of aliens had gathered around a holographic projection of the Earth, their features as varied as the stars. Tall, insectoid beings with iridescent wings stood beside reptilian creatures with scales that shimmered like liquid metal. Humanoid figures with elongated skulls and glowing eyes whispered in low tones.

At the center of the gathering stood a towering figure cloaked in shadows. Its voice was deep and commanding, resonating through the chamber.

"The Bug has retrieved the shard," the figure announced. "Soon, the dimensional rift will be complete, and Earth will be ours to divide."

K stiffened, his grip tightening on his weapon. "Looks like we found our conspiracy."

The Doctor held up a hand, signaling for silence. He crept closer to the group, using the shadows to his advantage. "Let's listen before we act," he whispered. "No need to crash the party prematurely."

The Plan Unveiled

The cloaked figure continued speaking, its tone dripping with authority. "The humans will be too distracted by the Bug's destruction to notice our true purpose. Once the rift is stable, we'll bring through reinforcements and claim the planet for our factions."

One of the insectoid aliens stepped forward, clicking its mandibles. "And the TARDIS? Are you certain it can be controlled?"

The cloaked figure hesitated for a moment before answering. "The TARDIS is the key. With its technology, we can stabilize the rift indefinitely. But the Doctor must not interfere. If he becomes a threat, we will eliminate him."

J leaned in, whispering to K. "They're talking about your boy over there. Think they can take him out?"

K smirked faintly. "They can try."

The Doctor turned back to them, his face unusually serious. "They're not just using the Bug for chaos—they're orchestrating a coordinated invasion. Multiple factions, working together. That's rare. Aliens don't usually play well with others."

"Why now?" K asked. "What's so special about Earth?"

The Doctor sighed. "Earth is special because of its potential. Its position in the universe, its resources, its people. Everyone wants a piece of it. And now, with the TARDIS in play, it's a prize too tempting to ignore."

The Confrontation

Before the group could retreat, one of the humanoid aliens turned, its glowing eyes locking onto the Doctor. It hissed something in its alien tongue, and the room fell silent as the gathered aliens turned to face the intruders.

"Ah," the Doctor said, stepping forward with a disarming smile. "Hello! I couldn't help but overhear your little plan. Very ambitious, I must say, but also very doomed to fail."

The cloaked figure stepped closer, its shadowy form looming over the Doctor. "You should not have come here, Time Lord. This is no concern of yours."

"Oh, but it is," the Doctor said, his voice sharp. "You're threatening Earth—my favorite planet, by the way—and you're endangering billions of lives. Not to mention, you're misusing my TARDIS, which is a very personal offense."

K and J stepped up beside the Doctor, their weapons drawn. J smirked. "Yeah, what he said. Now, how about you call off your Bug and pack it up before things get ugly?"

The figure chuckled, a deep, guttural sound. "You are too late. The Bug is already en route to the TARDIS. By the time you return, the rift will be open, and Earth will belong to us."

The Doctor's expression darkened, his voice dropping to a dangerous calm. "Oh, you really don't know who you're dealing with, do you?"

The figure raised a hand, and the gathered aliens advanced. The Doctor spun toward J and K. "Run!"

The Escape

The chamber erupted into chaos as the aliens charged. K and J opened fire, their energy weapons lighting up the cavern with green bursts. The Doctor darted toward the exit, dodging claws and beams of energy as he ran.

"This is why I hate conspiracies!" J shouted as he fired over his shoulder. "Too many bad guys, not enough exits!"

"Keep moving!" K barked, his aim precise as he took down an insectoid creature blocking their path.

The trio scrambled up the staircase, the sound of alien roars echoing behind them. As they burst back into the subway station, the Doctor slammed the maintenance door shut and sealed it with his sonic screwdriver.

"That won't hold them for long," the Doctor said, panting. "We need to get back to the TARDIS. If they reach her before we do—"

"They won't," K interrupted, already sprinting toward the TARDIS.

Back to the TARDIS

The group arrived at the TARDIS just as the ground began to tremble. The Bug's screech echoed in the distance, growing louder with each passing second.

The Doctor threw open the TARDIS doors and raced to the console. "We're out of time. J, K, get in here!"

The agents followed, slamming the doors shut behind them. The Doctor flipped switches and turned knobs, the TARDIS coming to life with a groan.

"We need to intercept the Bug before it reaches the TARDIS's dimensional core," the Doctor said, his hands moving frantically. "If they access it, the rift will destabilize, and Earth won't just be invaded—it'll be obliterated."

K nodded grimly. "Then let's stop it."

As the TARDIS dematerialized, the Doctor's voice rang out with fierce determination. "This conspiracy ends now."

Chapter 10: Into the Hive

The TARDIS materialized with its familiar wheeze deep underground, the vibrations from its arrival disturbing the eerie quiet. The Doctor, Agent J, and Agent K stepped out into a cavern illuminated by an unnatural green glow. The air was thick with humidity, and the faint, rhythmic sound of something pulsating echoed through the tunnels.

J wrinkled his nose. "Man, this place stinks. Like rotten eggs and bad decisions."

K glanced around, his weapon drawn. "Stay focused. This isn't just a hideout—it's a stronghold."

The Doctor moved ahead, his sonic screwdriver buzzing faintly as he scanned the environment. "Not just a stronghold," he said, his voice tinged with worry. "A hive."

J raised an eyebrow. "Hive? Like bees?"

"More like Bugs," the Doctor corrected, turning to face them. "And not just our oversized friend from the city. This is a breeding ground."

K's gaze hardened. "Breeding ground for what?"

The Doctor shined his screwdriver toward the tunnel ahead, revealing rows of translucent, gelatinous eggs lining the walls. Inside, dark, twitching shapes moved as if responding to the newcomers' presence.

"Those," the Doctor said grimly. "Hundreds of them. Maybe thousands deeper in. If they hatch—"

J cut him off. "Let me guess. Earth becomes Bug Central?"

"Precisely," the Doctor said, spinning on his heel. "And I'd wager whoever's controlling our big Bug upstairs is planning to use these hatchlings to solidify their invasion. A ready-made army, birthed right under your feet."

K stepped forward, his eyes scanning the eggs. "How much time do we have?"

The Doctor hesitated, scanning one of the eggs with his sonic screwdriver. "Not long. The pulsation you're hearing—that's a synchronization signal. They'll all hatch at once when it reaches its peak."

J groaned. "Of course. Because nothing's ever simple with you, Doc."

The Doctor ignored him, his mind already racing. "We need to find the central nexus. That's where the synchronization signal is being broadcast. Shut it down, and we can stop the hatching."

Navigating the Hive

The trio moved cautiously through the twisting tunnels, their footsteps muffled by the damp, spongy ground. The walls seemed to shimmer, covered in a slick, organic substance that pulsed faintly with life.

J kept glancing over his shoulder, muttering under his breath. "I swear I heard something."

K shot him a look. "Keep it together. These things don't scare easy."

"Yeah, well," J said, gripping his weapon tighter, "they don't have to. I'm doing enough scaring for all of us."

The Doctor stopped suddenly, holding up a hand. "Shh! Listen."

The group froze, straining to hear over the faint pulsations. A low, chittering sound echoed from deeper within the hive, growing louder with each passing second.

"Guards," the Doctor whispered, motioning for them to hide behind a cluster of boulders.

A pair of insectoid creatures skittered into view, their elongated limbs and sharp mandibles glinting in the green light. They moved with an unsettling grace, their multifaceted eyes scanning the tunnel.

J leaned close to the Doctor, his voice barely above a whisper. "Please tell me you've got a plan."

The Doctor grinned. "Of course. Improvisation."

J groaned. "That's not a plan!"

Before J could protest further, the Doctor stepped out from behind the boulders, his arms raised in a gesture of peace. "Hello! Lovely hive you've got here. Very atmospheric."

The creatures froze, their heads tilting in unison as they clicked their mandibles.

"I don't suppose you'd be willing to show me to your nexus, would you?" the Doctor continued, his tone casual.

The creatures let out a high-pitched screech and charged toward him.

"Guess that's a no," the Doctor muttered, darting back behind the boulders.

K and J opened fire, their weapons emitting bursts of green energy. The blasts struck the creatures, but their exoskeletons absorbed much of the impact, and they kept advancing.

"Doc!" J shouted. "A little help here?"

The Doctor pulled out his sonic screwdriver, adjusting the settings. "Hold them off for just a moment!" He aimed the screwdriver at the tunnel ceiling, and with a high-pitched whine, the organic substance above began to disintegrate, sending chunks of debris crashing down onto the guards.

The creatures screeched one last time before collapsing under the rubble.

"That should buy us some time," the Doctor said, brushing off his coat. "Come on, the nexus isn't far."

The Nexus Chamber

The trio entered a vast chamber at the heart of the hive. In the center stood a massive organic structure, pulsating with green light. Tendrils extended from it, connecting to the walls and ceiling like veins. The rhythmic sound of the synchronization signal was deafening here, and the Doctor's face turned grim.

"That's it," he said, pointing to the structure. "The nexus. It's controlling the entire hive."

K approached cautiously, his weapon ready. "How do we shut it down?"

The Doctor circled the nexus, his sonic screwdriver scanning the tendrils. "We need to overload the signal. If I can reverse the frequency, it'll disrupt the synchronization and halt the hatching process."

J frowned. "And what happens if you're wrong?"

The Doctor shot him a look. "Then we'll have a very large, very angry swarm of Bugs to deal with."

"Great," J muttered. "No pressure or anything."

The Doctor began working furiously, using his screwdriver to adjust the nexus's frequency. The pulsations grew erratic, the light flickering as the organic structure began to shake.

Suddenly, a deafening screech echoed through the chamber. The Bug—the same one they'd been chasing—burst into the room, its massive form barely fitting through the tunnel. It lunged toward the Doctor, its mandibles snapping.

"Doctor, move!" K shouted, firing at the Bug to draw its attention.

The Doctor ducked just in time, rolling across the floor and resuming his work. "Keep her busy! I'm almost there!"

J fired at the Bug's legs, trying to slow it down. "We're trying, Doc, but she's not exactly cooperating!"

The Bug let out another screech, swiping at K and J with its claws. They dove out of the way, barely avoiding the attack.

"Done!" the Doctor shouted, flipping a final switch on his screwdriver.

The nexus let out a high-pitched whine before exploding in a burst of green energy. The pulsations stopped, and the hive fell eerily silent.

The Bug froze mid-attack, its body trembling as the signal controlling it faded. It let out a low, mournful sound before retreating into the shadows.

"What just happened?" J asked, lowering his weapon.

"I severed the signal," the Doctor explained, panting. "She's free now. No more control, no more hive."

K stepped forward, his expression unreadable. "And the eggs?"

The Doctor nodded toward the chamber walls, where the eggs had gone dark. "Dormant. Without the synchronization signal, they won't hatch."

J let out a relieved laugh. "We actually did it."

The Doctor smiled, though his eyes were somber. "For now. But whoever orchestrated this won't stop here. We've cut off one head of the hydra, but the others are still out there."

K nodded. "Then we'll be ready."

As they made their way back to the TARDIS, the Doctor couldn't shake the feeling that the conspiracy ran deeper than they'd uncovered. But for now, Earth was safe, and that was enough.

Chapter 11: The Doctor's Plan

Back aboard the **TARDIS**, the Doctor worked feverishly at the console, flipping switches, twisting knobs, and muttering to himself. The central column glowed steadily, the soft hum of the ship a stark contrast to the tension in the air. Agent J leaned against the wall, arms crossed, while K stood a few feet away, watching the Doctor's frenetic movements with his usual stoic demeanor.

"Alright, Doc," J said finally, breaking the silence. "You've been twiddling knobs and making the lights blink for a good ten minutes now. Care to let us in on your master plan?"

The Doctor straightened, spinning around with his signature grin. "Master plan? Oh, I like that! Yes, let's call it a master plan. You see, the Bug—our rather large, mandible-snapping friend—is still a threat. Even though we stopped the hive and severed the synchronization signal, she's got one last ace up her exoskeletal sleeve."

K stepped forward, his brow furrowed. "The TARDIS."

"Precisely," the Doctor said, pointing a finger at him. "She's been programmed—or rather, controlled—to reach the TARDIS at all costs. Why? Because with the TARDIS, she can stabilize the dimensional rift. That would make it possible to bring through whatever nasty invasion force her masters have lined up."

J frowned. "And you're saying we can't just stop her the old-fashioned way? You know, lasers, explosions, that kind of thing?"

The Doctor's smile faded, his tone turning serious. "We've tried that, J. The Bug isn't just any alien creature. She's been genetically enhanced, augmented for durability. And even if we could stop her, the damage she'd cause on the way to the TARDIS would be catastrophic."

K's voice was calm but firm. "So, what's your plan?"

The Doctor spun back to the console, pulling up a holographic projection of the Bug and the dimensional rift. "We're going to trap her in a parallel dimension."

J blinked. "A parallel what now?"

"A parallel dimension!" the Doctor repeated, gesturing dramatically to the projection. "Think of it as a pocket universe—a place where she can't escape, can't harm anyone, and can't be used as a pawn by her masters. It's a safe, contained solution."

K folded his arms. "And how do you propose we do that?"

The Doctor grinned, leaning over the console. "With a dimensional pulse. I can use the TARDIS to generate a focused burst of dimensional energy. It'll destabilize the Bug's current reality anchor—you know, the thing keeping her tethered to this universe—and pull her into the pocket dimension."

"Sounds great," J said, raising a hand. "But there's gotta be a catch. There's always a catch with you."

The Doctor's grin faltered slightly. "Well, yes, a teeny-tiny catch. For the pulse to work, we'll need to lure the Bug into an open area, somewhere the TARDIS can project the energy without interference. And we'll need to keep her occupied long enough for the pulse to build."

"How long?" K asked, his tone flat.

The Doctor winced. "Oh, just... five minutes or so."

J threw up his hands. "Five minutes? You want us to play bait for a twenty-foot murder Bug for five minutes? Are you out of your mind?"

"Not out of my mind, no," the Doctor said, his grin returning. "Just extremely clever. Besides, you'll have the MIB's finest technology at your disposal, and I'll be coordinating everything from the TARDIS. It's practically foolproof!"

K raised an eyebrow. "Practically?"

The Doctor waved a hand dismissively. "Details, details. The important thing is that it'll work."

The Doctor's Proposal

The group reconvened in the MIB command center, where Agent Zed sat at the head of the table, his steely gaze fixed on the Doctor. Holographic projections of the Bug and the TARDIS hovered above the table, and technicians worked tirelessly in the background.

"Let me get this straight," Zed said, his voice calm but skeptical. "You want us to lure this thing out, distract it for five minutes, and trust you to zap it into another dimension?"

The Doctor clapped his hands together. "Exactly! See, you've got it already. I knew you were sharp."

Zed wasn't amused. "And what happens if this plan of yours doesn't work?"

The Doctor leaned forward, his tone softening. "Then the Bug reaches the TARDIS. The rift opens. Earth becomes a warzone for invading alien factions. Millions—no, billions—of lives are at risk. I don't think any of us want that, do we?"

Zed studied him for a long moment before turning to K and J. "What do you two think?"

K's expression was unreadable. "It's risky, but it's the best option we've got. The Doctor's track record speaks for itself."

J shrugged. "Yeah, he's nuts, but his plans tend to work. Mostly."

Zed sighed heavily, leaning back in his chair. "Alright, Doctor. You've got our support. But you'd better not screw this up."

The Doctor beamed. "Oh, Zed, you won't regret this. Probably."

Preparing the Trap

Back in the TARDIS, the Doctor worked alongside MIB technicians to coordinate the dimensional pulse. Meanwhile, K and J assembled a team of agents armed with the MIB's most advanced weapons and gadgets. The chosen location was an abandoned industrial yard on the city's outskirts—spacious, isolated, and perfect for the TARDIS to deploy its energy pulse.

As they finalized preparations, J approached the Doctor. "You sure about this, Doc? This thing feels... big. Bigger than us."

The Doctor looked up from the console, his expression uncharacteristically serious. "It is big, J. But big things don't always need big solutions. Sometimes, it just takes a bit of cleverness and a lot of bravery."

J nodded, though his uncertainty lingered. "Alright. Let's hope you're as clever as you say."

The Doctor grinned. "Oh, I'm more than clever. I'm brilliant."

The Stage Is Set

As the TARDIS materialized at the industrial yard, the team prepared for the final confrontation. The Bug's screeches echoed in the distance, growing louder as it approached.

The Doctor adjusted the TARDIS's controls, his face alight with determination. "This is it, everyone. Once the pulse begins, there's no turning back. Stay sharp, stay focused, and stay alive."

The Bug's massive form appeared on the horizon, its multifaceted eyes glinting in the dim light. It let out an earth-shaking roar as it charged toward the TARDIS.

"Showtime," J muttered, raising his weapon.

"Let's give her a proper send-off," the Doctor said, flipping the final switch. The TARDIS began to hum with power, and the ground beneath them trembled.

The final battle had begun.

Chapter 12: Return of the TARDIS

The Doctor stood in the MIB command center, arms crossed, his eyes fixed on Agent Zed. The holographic map above the table displayed the industrial yard where the Bug would make its final move, glowing red with urgent energy spikes. Around the room, agents murmured as they exchanged updates, but the tension in the air was palpable.

"You need me, Zed," the Doctor said, his voice calm but insistent. "The TARDIS is the only thing standing between Earth and an interdimensional disaster. You've done your job. Now let me do mine."

Zed leaned back in his chair, steepling his fingers as he regarded the Doctor with a skeptical gaze. "And what happens after this, Doctor? You take your blue box and disappear? Leave us to clean up the mess?"

The Doctor tilted his head, his expression softening. "I'm not your enemy. I've protected this planet more times than I can count. But right now, you need to trust me. The TARDIS isn't just a ship; she's my partner. Together, we can end this."

K stepped forward, his tone measured. "Zed, the Doctor's plan is the best chance we've got. If we keep the TARDIS locked up, we lose Earth. Simple as that."

J nodded. "Yeah, and I don't know about you, but I'm not ready to start filling out my alien overlord compliance paperwork."

Zed sighed heavily, rubbing his temples. "Alright, Doctor. You get your ship back. But we're not letting you vanish without a trace." He gestured to one of the technicians. "Install a tracking device on the TARDIS. If the Doctor decides to go rogue, we'll know where to find him."

The Doctor raised an eyebrow. "A tracker? Oh, Zed, you don't trust easily, do you?"

"Not when the stakes are this high," Zed replied, his tone firm. "Take it or leave it."

The Doctor thought for a moment before shrugging with a grin. "Fine. Install your little tracker. But don't be surprised if it has a bit of trouble keeping up."

Reunited with the TARDIS

In the containment bay, the TARDIS stood motionless, her blue exterior dim and silent. The Doctor approached slowly, running a hand along the wooden panels. His expression was one of deep relief, as if reuniting with an old friend.

"Hello, old girl," he murmured. "Miss me?"

The central light atop the TARDIS blinked faintly, as if in response.

The MIB technicians worked quickly, affixing a small, sleek tracking device to the exterior of the ship. The Doctor watched with mild amusement, leaning against the TARDIS door.

"You know," he said, "she's going to shake that off the moment she feels like it. The TARDIS doesn't like being told what to do."

J smirked. "Sounds like someone else I know."

K ignored the banter, stepping closer to the Doctor. "We're trusting you with this, Doctor. Don't make us regret it."

The Doctor nodded, his expression uncharacteristically serious. "I won't. You have my word."

With that, he unlocked the TARDIS door and stepped inside. The familiar hum of the central console greeted him, and a wave of calm washed over him.

"Right," he said, rubbing his hands together. "Let's get to work."

Coordinating with the MIB

Inside the TARDIS, the Doctor activated the holographic interface, connecting the ship's systems to the MIB's network. The command center appeared as a shimmering projection in the center of the console room, where Zed, K, and J could see the Doctor.

"Alright," the Doctor began, pointing to a rotating model of the Bug. "Here's the plan. The TARDIS will generate a dimensional pulse to trap the Bug in a parallel dimension. But to do that, we need to lure her into the open and keep her there for at least five minutes."

Zed frowned. "Five minutes is a long time in a fight."

"Yes, but it's what we need," the Doctor said. "The TARDIS can create a containment field around the pulse, but if the Bug moves outside of it, the entire operation fails."

K nodded. "We'll keep her in range. What else?"

The Doctor gestured to a map of the industrial yard. "I'll position the TARDIS here, at the center of the pulse. Your job is to keep her attention on you while I initiate the sequence. Once the pulse begins, it can't be stopped."

J groaned. "So we're playing bait. Again."

"Think of it as a distraction," the Doctor said with a grin. "A very important distraction. Oh, and try not to get eaten."

"Not funny," J muttered.

K's voice was steady. "We'll hold the line. Just make sure you do your part."

Final Preparations

As the TARDIS dematerialized and reappeared at the industrial yard, the MIB team mobilized, setting up defensive positions and deploying energy barriers. The Doctor emerged from the TARDIS, his sonic screwdriver in hand, directing agents to their posts.

"Remember," he called out, "the Bug's primary instinct is to reach the TARDIS. Use that to your advantage. Keep her focused, keep her moving, and whatever you do, don't let her near the ship."

J adjusted his weapon, glancing at K. "You think he's gonna pull this off?"

K didn't answer immediately, his gaze fixed on the Doctor. "He's got the TARDIS back. Let's hope that's enough."

The Doctor clapped his hands together, his voice cutting through the tension. "Alright, everyone! Places! The star of the show is on her way, and we've got one chance to get this right."

As the ground began to tremble and the distant screech of the Bug echoed closer, the Doctor retreated into the TARDIS, ready to initiate the dimensional pulse. With the MIB's trust—and Earth's future—on the line, the stage was set for the final confrontation.

Chapter 13: A Bug in the System

The MIB command center was a flurry of activity as agents prepared for the final confrontation with the Bug. Energy weapons were charged, containment protocols reviewed, and tactical teams deployed to key locations around the industrial yard. The Doctor paced in front of a holographic projection of the area, briefing K and J on the finer points of his dimensional pulse plan.

"And remember," the Doctor said, gesturing emphatically, "the TARDIS will project the pulse, but we need to keep her stationary and the Bug inside the containment field long enough for it to activate. No interruptions, no distractions—"

The ground beneath their feet suddenly shuddered violently, cutting him off mid-sentence. Alarms blared, and the holographic map flickered as the room was plunged into chaos.

"What the hell was that?" J shouted, grabbing his weapon.

Zed's voice boomed over the intercom. "Security breach! The Bug's in the building!"

The Doctor froze, his face darkening. "In the building? How—?"

Another quake rocked the command center, sending agents stumbling. The lights flickered, and an eerie screech echoed through the hallways, unmistakable in its ferocity. The Bug had arrived.

The Bug Takes Control

The group sprinted toward the containment bay, where the TARDIS was stationed. The Doctor led the way, his sonic screwdriver illuminating the dim, flickering corridors.

"It's her," the Doctor said breathlessly. "She's been tracking the TARDIS this whole time. The industrial yard was a diversion—her real target was always the ship!"

K kept his weapon ready, his jaw clenched. "Then why didn't you see this coming?"

"Because," the Doctor snapped, "she's smarter than we gave her credit for."

As they reached the containment bay, the sight before them stopped them in their tracks. The Bug stood at the TARDIS's door, her massive claws tearing through the last remnants of the containment field. Sparks flew as the security systems failed, and with a final screech, she forced the doors open and stepped inside.

"No!" the Doctor shouted, running toward the TARDIS. "She'll destabilize everything!"

The Bug disappeared into the blue box, her massive form vanishing into the impossible interior. Without hesitation, the Doctor followed, K and J close behind.

Trapped Inside the TARDIS

Inside, the TARDIS was unrecognizable. The familiar hum of the console room had been replaced by a discordant, grating noise. The glowing pillars flickered erratically, casting the room in an unsettling light. The Bug's claws had ripped through several of the TARDIS's delicate panels, exposing wires and alien circuitry that sparked dangerously.

"She's interfering with the dimensional controls," the Doctor muttered, his voice tinged with panic. "If she keeps this up, she'll tear the TARDIS apart—and take us with it!"

The Bug let out another screech, its massive form perched precariously near the central console. Its multifaceted eyes glowed with a strange, unnatural light.

J raised his weapon. "I can take the shot."

"Don't!" the Doctor shouted, stepping in front of him. "You could damage the TARDIS. We need to outthink her, not blast her."

K scanned the room, his sharp eyes taking in the chaos. "Then what's the plan, Doctor?"

The Doctor spun to the console, his fingers flying over the controls. "She's connected to the shard—still carrying its energy. That's how she's able to interact with the TARDIS. If I can isolate her signal, I might be able to trap her in a containment loop within the ship."

"And if you can't?" K asked grimly.

The Doctor didn't look up. "Then she destabilizes the core, and we all get scattered across time and space. Forever."

The Deadly Game

The TARDIS shuddered violently as the Bug lunged toward the Doctor, her claws narrowly missing him as he dove behind the console. K and J fired carefully, their blasts hitting the walls near the Bug to distract it without damaging the ship further.

"Keep her away from the console!" the Doctor shouted, recalibrating the containment systems. "If she accesses the dimensional controls, she could open a rift inside the TARDIS!"

J ducked behind a pillar, shouting over the chaos. "Doc, I don't know how long we can keep this up!"

The Bug screeched, its movements erratic as it tore through the room, smashing pillars and sending shards of glowing debris flying.

The Doctor adjusted his sonic screwdriver, aiming it at the Bug. A high-pitched frequency emitted from the device, causing the Bug to pause, her movements slowing as she writhed in discomfort.

"That's it," the Doctor muttered, his eyes locked on the creature. "The shard's energy is disrupting her connection. If I can amplify the pulse—"

The Bug, sensing the threat, turned her attention back to the Doctor and lunged. K fired a shot that grazed her side, forcing her to veer off course.

"Nice shot," J said, nodding to K.

K didn't reply, his focus unbroken.

The Final Move

The Doctor worked furiously, his fingers flying over the console. "Just a few more seconds," he muttered. "Come on, come on—"

The TARDIS groaned as a containment field began to form around the Bug, glowing tendrils of light spiraling upward to encase her. The creature screeched in rage, clawing at the energy, but her movements grew slower as the field solidified.

"It's working!" J shouted, stepping out from cover.

"Don't celebrate yet!" the Doctor warned. "The containment field is unstable. If she breaks out—"

The TARDIS shuddered again, the lights dimming as the containment field pulsed erratically. The Doctor spun to face K and J. "I need you to hold her attention just a little longer. I have to reroute power to stabilize the field!"

K nodded, his weapon ready. "We've got this."

As the Doctor dove back into the console, K and J opened fire, their blasts carefully aimed to keep the Bug at bay without disrupting the containment field. The creature's screeches filled the air as it lashed out, but the energy tendrils began to tighten, binding it in place.

"Got it!" the Doctor shouted, slamming a lever into place. The containment field flared brightly, and with a final pulse, the Bug was frozen, her massive form encased in glowing energy.

The room fell silent, save for the faint hum of the TARDIS's systems. The Doctor straightened, wiping his brow as he stared at the contained Bug.

"That," he said, exhaling deeply, "was far too close."

Aftermath

As the TARDIS's systems began to stabilize, the Doctor turned to K and J. "We've trapped her in a dimensional pocket within the TARDIS. She's harmless now—at least until we figure out what to do with her."

J leaned against a pillar, his weapon still in hand. "Man, I need a vacation."

K glanced at the Doctor. "What about the shard? Is it still a threat?"

The Doctor nodded. "It's still connected to her, but with the TARDIS's containment systems, it won't cause any more damage. For now."

Zed's voice crackled through the communicator. "Doctor, agents, report."

The Doctor smiled faintly, glancing at his companions. "Tell him the Bug's been neutralized. For good this time."

K nodded, stepping aside to deliver the report. J gave the Doctor a tired grin. "You really know how to make a mess, Doc."

The Doctor's grin returned, though his eyes carried a hint of sadness. "It's not about the mess, J. It's about cleaning it up."

As the TARDIS hummed softly around them, the Doctor knew the battle wasn't over. The Bug's masters were still out there, and the fight for Earth's safety was far from finished. But for now, they'd won—and that was enough.

Chapter 14: Time-Loop Trap

The TARDIS shuddered violently, its interior lights flickering as the containment field surrounding the Bug pulsed erratically. The Doctor, K, and J stood near the central console, their expressions tense as the air around them grew heavy with static.

"Doctor," K said sharply, his eyes fixed on the Bug's glowing containment, "what's happening?"

The Doctor darted around the console, his sonic screwdriver buzzing as he scanned the room. "She's done something," he muttered, his voice tinged with frustration. "The shard's energy—it's resonating with the TARDIS's systems. She's destabilizing the temporal matrix!"

J raised an eyebrow. "In English, Doc?"

The Doctor looked up, his face grim. "She's creating a time loop. If she succeeds, we'll be stuck repeating the same moment over and over again—trapped inside the TARDIS, while she uses the loop to learn how to access the dimensional core."

Before anyone could respond, the room flickered and went dark for a split second. When the lights returned, everything was eerily still.

The First Loop

The Doctor froze, his gaze darting around the room. "Did you feel that?"

"Feel what?" J asked, confused.

K's eyes narrowed. "We're back where we started."

The Doctor spun to the console, his hands flying over the controls. "Oh no. Oh no, no, no. It's already begun."

J stepped forward. "Wait, hold up. What do you mean? We're still here, right?"

"Yes, but we've already done this," the Doctor said, pointing to the Bug. "Look at her containment field—it's resetting. The energy buildup we just saw is starting over."

K looked at the field and then at the Doctor. "How do we stop it?"

The Doctor glanced at them, his face serious. "We figure out the trigger. Every loop has a pattern, a weak point. If we find it, we can break free."

The Second Loop

The TARDIS flickered again, and suddenly, they were back in the same positions as before: the Doctor at the console, K standing near the containment field, and J pacing near a pillar.

"Here we go again," the Doctor muttered, immediately scanning the room with his screwdriver.

"Okay, this is seriously weird," J said, spinning in place. "I was just here. I just said that!"

"Yes, J," the Doctor replied, his tone clipped. "And you'll keep saying it until we stop her."

The Bug let out a low, guttural screech, and the containment field flared briefly before dimming.

K's gaze locked onto the creature. "She's learning. Each time we reset, she gets closer to breaking out."

"Exactly," the Doctor said, typing furiously on the console. "She's using the loop to probe the TARDIS's defenses, testing for weaknesses. If we don't stop her soon, she'll figure out how to access the dimensional controls."

The Third Loop

This time, the Doctor was ready. As soon as the loop reset, he shouted, "Listen to me! We're in a time loop, and every iteration, she's getting closer. We need to change something—anything—to disrupt the pattern."

J looked skeptical. "Change what? She's in a box! We're in a box! What else can we do?"

The Doctor paused, considering. "The loop is tied to the shard's energy signature. She's using it to anchor the reset point. If we can disrupt her connection to the shard, we might be able to break the loop."

K nodded. "How do we do that?"

The Doctor's eyes lit up. "We overload it. The shard is unstable—it thrives on balance. If we introduce an opposite frequency, it could destabilize the entire loop."

J frowned. "And by 'destabilize,' you mean...?"

The Doctor hesitated. "There's a chance the loop collapses completely, taking us with it. But it's better than being stuck here forever while she learns how to destroy the universe."

J groaned. "Great. Love those odds."

The Fourth Loop

The flicker came again, and they were back. This time, the Doctor moved with purpose, pulling wires from the TARDIS console and linking them to his sonic screwdriver. Sparks flew as he adjusted the settings, creating a small, glowing orb of energy.

"What's that?" K asked, his tone calm despite the chaos.

"A counter-frequency generator," the Doctor said, his voice hurried. "It'll cancel out the shard's energy and force the loop to collapse."

J glanced at the Bug, whose claws scraped ominously against the containment field. "And how do we know this won't just make things worse?"

The Doctor grinned, his manic energy returning. "We don't!"

"Fantastic," J muttered.

The Bug let out another screech, its movements more aggressive as the containment field flickered dangerously. The Doctor finished his adjustments and turned to K and J.

"Get ready," he said, holding up the generator. "Once I activate this, the loop will fight back. Things are going to get... wibbly."

"Wibbly?" J asked, incredulous.

"Very wibbly," the Doctor confirmed, pressing a button on the generator.

Breaking the Loop

The room trembled violently as the counter-frequency clashed with the shard's energy. The lights flickered wildly, and the TARDIS's central column glowed brighter than ever before. The Bug screeched in fury, thrashing against the containment field as it began to destabilize.

"Hold on!" the Doctor shouted, gripping the console as the room seemed to twist and warp around them.

J clung to a nearby pillar. "This better work, Doc!"

K stood firm, his weapon trained on the Bug. "What happens if it doesn't?"

The Doctor grinned, even as the room spun around them. "Then we'll have an eternity to figure it out!"

With a final, deafening pulse, the containment field collapsed, and the shard emitted a blinding light. The TARDIS groaned as the energy surge filled the room, and then—

Silence.

The Loop is Broken

The Doctor opened his eyes slowly, finding himself slumped against the console. The room was quiet, the hum of the TARDIS steady and calm once more. He stood, brushing himself off, and looked around.

J groaned from where he lay sprawled on the floor. "Did we make it? Are we out?"

K was already on his feet, scanning the room. "Looks like it."

The Doctor grinned, clapping his hands together. "Yes! We did it! The loop is broken, the shard's neutralized, and the Bug—" He turned to where the containment field had been, now empty. "Oh."

J sat up, his eyes widening. "Oh? What do you mean, 'oh'?"

The Doctor scratched the back of his head, his grin turning sheepish. "She's gone. Escaped into the TARDIS somewhere. But don't worry! She's trapped inside the ship. We'll find her."

K sighed. "One problem at a time, Doctor."

The Doctor nodded, his eyes sparkling with determination. "Right. Let's go Bug hunting, shall we?"

Chapter 15: Breaking the Loop

The TARDIS groaned under the strain of the time loop, its once steady hum now replaced with erratic pulsations. The Doctor darted around the central console, his brow furrowed in concentration as his hands flew over the controls. The loop had intensified, resetting faster with each cycle, and the Bug was becoming increasingly adept at navigating the TARDIS's systems.

"Doctor," K said, his voice steady despite the chaos, "you said we'd find the Bug in the last loop. What happened?"

"We did find her," the Doctor replied, his tone clipped. "And then we lost her again. She's clever—cleverer than I anticipated. But I think I know what she's doing now."

"Enlighten us," J said, gripping a railing as the TARDIS shuddered violently. "Because I'm getting real tired of being on repeat."

The Doctor spun to face them, his eyes alight with realization. "She's using the TARDIS's temporal engines to fuel the loop! The shard gave her the initial energy, but now she's tapped into the ship itself. She's piggybacking off the TARDIS's power, using it to maintain the loop and learn more with each reset."

K frowned. "And if she keeps at it?"

The Doctor's expression darkened. "If she gains full control of the temporal engines, she could expand the loop beyond the TARDIS—trap the entire planet, maybe even the galaxy, in a repeating fragment of time. Infinite resets, infinite chaos."

J groaned. "Great. So how do we stop her?"

The Doctor turned back to the console, adjusting the controls with precision. "By reversing the polarity of the temporal engines. It'll disrupt her connection and collapse the loop entirely."

"That sounds easy," J said, a note of suspicion in his voice. "Too easy."

The Doctor glanced at him, a wry smile tugging at his lips. "Oh, it's not easy. Reversing the polarity will create a massive temporal shockwave. The TARDIS will survive—it always does—but the feedback could eject us into random points in time and space. And there's also the slight possibility it could destroy the engines altogether."

"'Slight possibility'?" K repeated, his tone icy.

The Doctor shrugged. "Oh, you know, fifty-fifty. Give or take."

"Fantastic," J muttered. "Well, what are we waiting for?"

Preparing the Engines

The Doctor led K and J to the TARDIS's temporal engine room, a sprawling chamber filled with glowing orbs and interwoven streams of light that pulsed rhythmically. The engines, normally serene, now sparked and flickered with chaotic energy. The Bug's influence was unmistakable—her claw marks marred the walls, and faint traces of her screeches echoed through the room.

"There she is," the Doctor muttered, pointing to a massive conduit in the center of the room. Tendrils of glowing energy snaked toward the ceiling, pulsating in time with the loop resets. "She's latched onto the engine core. That's her anchor."

K surveyed the room, his weapon at the ready. "How do we get her off it?"

"Carefully," the Doctor replied, already pulling out his sonic screwdriver. "I'll reverse the polarity manually, but you two need to keep her busy. Distract her long enough for me to finish."

J raised an eyebrow. "Distract her? Doc, she's twenty feet tall and pissed off. What exactly are we supposed to do—sing her a lullaby?"

The Doctor grinned. "Oh, be creative. Bugs are surprisingly impressionable."

K's voice was calm but firm. "We'll handle it. Just do your part."

The Bug Strikes

As the Doctor began his adjustments, the Bug emerged from the shadows, her massive form casting an ominous silhouette across the room. Her screech was deafening, and her claws scraped against the metal floor as she charged toward the engine core.

"Now would be a good time to distract her!" the Doctor shouted over the noise.

K and J sprang into action, firing their energy weapons at the Bug. The blasts struck her exoskeleton, forcing her to slow but not stopping her completely.

"She's getting closer!" J yelled, diving behind a console as the Bug's claws swiped inches from him.

K fired a precision shot at one of the tendrils connecting the Bug to the core. The tendril sparked and recoiled, causing the Bug to shriek in pain and turn her attention to him.

"Over here!" K shouted, moving to draw the Bug away from the core.

The Doctor worked furiously, his sonic screwdriver emitting a steady whine as he rerouted power and adjusted the polarity settings. "Just a little longer!" he called out.

The Bug, enraged, slammed her claws into the floor, sending a shockwave that knocked J off his feet. "We don't have a little longer!" J shouted, scrambling to his feet.

The Temporal Shockwave

"Done!" the Doctor shouted triumphantly, flipping a final switch on the engine console. The room shook violently as the reversed polarity surged through the temporal engines. The glowing tendrils connecting the Bug to the core snapped, and she let out a piercing scream as she was thrown backward.

The engines emitted a blinding flash of light, and the TARDIS groaned as the temporal loop collapsed. For a moment, everything was still.

J coughed, brushing debris off his jacket. "Did we do it?"

The Doctor stood, dusting himself off. "We did it. The loop is broken."

K scanned the room, his weapon still at the ready. "Where's the Bug?"

Before the Doctor could answer, a loud crash echoed from the engine room's far end. A massive hole had been torn into the TARDIS wall, leading into open air. Beyond it was the glittering skyline of the city—the Bug had escaped.

The Doctor's face fell. "Oh, that's not good."

J stared at the hole in disbelief. "You're telling me she just tore through the TARDIS and bailed?"

"She used the temporal shockwave to piggyback out," the Doctor said, running a hand through his hair. "Clever girl."

K's voice was sharp. "Where is she now?"

The Doctor adjusted his sonic screwdriver, scanning the cityscape. "She's in the heart of the city. And she's angrier than ever."

A New Threat

The trio returned to the TARDIS console room, where the Doctor worked quickly to track the Bug's movements. "She's heading for a convergence point—a place where the dimensional rift is still weak. If she gets there, she could reopen the rift and bring her masters through."

J groaned. "I thought we stopped the loop to prevent this."

"We did," the Doctor replied, his tone clipped. "But she's persistent. She knows the TARDIS can stop her, so she's forcing our hand."

K's voice was steady. "What's the plan, Doctor?"

The Doctor looked up, his expression resolute. "We face her head-on. No more loops, no more games. This ends now."

With the TARDIS's engines stabilized and the city at stake, the Doctor and the MIB prepared for their final confrontation with the Bug—a battle that would decide the fate of Earth once and for all.

Chapter 16: The Final Warning

The **TARDIS** hummed steadily in the heart of the MIB command center, where the Doctor, Agent K, Agent J, and Zed stood before a holographic projection of New York City. Pulsing red markers indicated energy spikes radiating across the grid, converging on a single glowing dot near Midtown.

"This is it," the Doctor said, his voice tight with urgency as he pointed to the map. "She's heading for the city's primary energy hub—your central nexus for power distribution. And it's not just electricity; it's a convergence of ley lines, residual cosmic energy, and, conveniently for her, dimensional interference from the shard."

Zed leaned forward, his face grim. "And if she gets there?"

The Doctor turned to him, his expression unusually serious. "If she reaches the hub, she'll have everything she needs to open the dimensional rift. With the shard acting as a stabilizer and the energy from the hub amplifying it, the rift won't just be a doorway—it'll be a gaping wound in the fabric of reality. Her masters won't just send reinforcements; they'll pour through in droves, turning Earth into a staging ground for an interdimensional war."

K's jaw tightened. "How long do we have?"

The Doctor tapped his sonic screwdriver against the console, his brow furrowed. "At her current speed? Less than an hour."

J let out a low whistle. "And I'm guessing this isn't one of those problems we can solve with a really big bug zapper."

"Not unless your bug zapper can neutralize interdimensional anomalies," the Doctor quipped, flashing a grim smile. "But that doesn't mean we're out of options. If we can intercept her before she reaches the hub, we might stand a chance."

Zed straightened, his voice cutting through the tension. "We're mobilizing every available agent. Doctor, you've got the TARDIS. What do you need from us?"

The Plan

The room bustled with activity as the Doctor outlined his strategy. Holographic projections flickered in the air as agents reviewed blueprints of the energy hub and the surrounding streets.

"The hub is heavily fortified," K said, pointing to a network of access points on the map. "But if the Bug is as smart as you say, she'll find the weakest link and force her way in."

"Exactly," the Doctor said, pacing in front of the group. "That's why we're going to force her to play by our rules. We need to set up a perimeter—layers of defenses to slow her down. Every second we buy is another second we can use to stabilize the dimensional breach she's trying to create."

J frowned. "And how are we supposed to stop her? You saw her. She took out half the TARDIS without breaking a sweat."

The Doctor paused, turning to face him. "She's fast, she's strong, and she's determined. But she's also predictable. She wants the hub, and she's single-minded in her pursuit. That's her weakness. If we can anticipate her moves, we can funnel her into a trap."

Zed nodded. "What kind of trap?"

The Doctor grinned, his eyes sparkling with determination. "An energy containment field. Big, powerful, and calibrated to her unique signature. I can modify the TARDIS to project it, but I'll need your agents to keep her within the containment zone long enough for it to activate."

K crossed his arms. "And if she breaks out?"

The Doctor's smile faltered. "Then we're out of tricks, and she wins."

Mobilizing the MIB

MIB vehicles roared to life, their sleek black designs cutting through the city streets like shadows. Agents in full tactical gear deployed at key points around the energy hub, setting up barriers, energy cannons, and containment nodes. The Doctor oversaw the preparations from the TARDIS, his hands flying over the console as he calibrated the containment field.

J paced near the console, his weapon slung over his shoulder. "You sure about this, Doc? I mean, I get the whole 'genius Time Lord' thing, but this is starting to feel like a suicide mission."

The Doctor looked up, his expression softer. "It's not suicide, J. It's survival. For you, for me, for everyone on this planet. If we don't stop her now, there won't be another chance."

J sighed, leaning against the railing. "You ever think about why you do this? Running around the universe, saving people who barely know you exist?"

The Doctor smiled faintly. "Every day. But if I didn't, who would?"

The Bug's Arrival

The ground trembled as the Bug emerged from the shadows of the city, her massive form silhouetted against the flickering streetlights. Her screeches echoed through the air, sending chills down the spines of the agents standing their ground.

"She's here," K said into his communicator, his voice steady. "All units, hold positions. Don't engage until the Doctor gives the signal."

The Bug charged toward the first line of defenses, her claws tearing through barriers as if they were paper. Energy blasts struck her exoskeleton, slowing her slightly but doing little to stop her advance.

"Doctor," Zed's voice came over the TARDIS speakers, "we're losing ground. How much longer?"

The Doctor adjusted a lever, his expression tight with focus. "Just a few more minutes. Keep her occupied!"

The Final Warning

The Bug reached the second line of defenses, her movements more calculated as she adapted to the agents' strategies. K and J led a team to flank her, firing precision shots at her legs to slow her down.

"This isn't working!" J shouted. "She's still heading for the hub!"

The Doctor's voice crackled over their earpieces. "She's almost in position. Just a little longer!"

The Bug let out a deafening screech and surged forward, breaking through the final barricade. The energy hub loomed ahead, its towering structure glowing with raw power.

"Doctor!" K barked. "She's at the hub. We're out of time."

Inside the TARDIS, the Doctor slammed a lever into place. The central column glowed brighter than ever, and a beam of light shot out from the ship, creating a shimmering containment field around the Bug.

"Got her!" the Doctor shouted triumphantly. "The field is holding!"

The Race Against Time

The Bug thrashed against the containment field, her claws sparking as they struck the energy barrier. The shard embedded in her chest began to glow, resonating with the energy of the hub.

"She's trying to overload the field," the Doctor muttered, his hands flying over the console. "If she succeeds, the rift will tear open."

J's voice came through the communicator. "Then what do we do?"

The Doctor's face hardened. "We finish this. For good."

As the Bug pushed against the containment field, the Doctor prepared for one final move—a gambit that would determine the fate of Earth and everyone on it.

Chapter 17: The Alien Alliance

The Bug's containment field glowed with a faint, unsteady pulse as it thrashed against its restraints. The Doctor paced in front of the TARDIS console, furiously scanning the city with his sonic screwdriver. Nearby, J and K exchanged uneasy glances as they watched the holographic map projected above the console. Red blips were multiplying rapidly across the city, each representing a new disturbance.

"Doctor," K said, his voice as calm as ever, "what are we looking at here?"

The Doctor glanced up, his face grim. "We're looking at coordinated chaos. The Bug's not working alone—it never was."

J pointed at the map, where several hotspots had appeared around major city landmarks. "You mean these other blips? They're her buddies?"

The Doctor nodded. "Exactly. A group of rogue aliens—her allies—are using the chaos of her escape to launch their own attack. They're targeting the city's critical infrastructure, creating distractions to pull your agents away from the energy hub."

Zed's voice crackled over the TARDIS speakers. "Doctor, we've got reports of alien incursions all over the city. Subway collapses, power outages, even an attack near the mayor's office. My agents are spread too thin."

The Doctor sighed, running a hand through his hair. "That's the point, Zed. Divide and conquer. If you don't respond, the city falls into chaos. If you do, the Bug has free rein to focus on the rift."

J threw up his hands. "So what do we do? We can't be everywhere at once!"

The Doctor snapped his fingers. "But we can be efficient. We split up. You and K handle the ground threats while I stabilize the Bug's containment field. Once the immediate danger is under control, we regroup to deal with the big one."

K frowned, his tone skeptical. "You're suggesting we leave the most dangerous threat—the Bug—here with you, alone?"

The Doctor grinned. "What can I say? I thrive under pressure."

Splitting Up

The TARDIS materialized near City Hall, where one of the largest disturbances was underway. The building's grand facade was partially crumbled, and a group of sleek, insectoid aliens armed with advanced weaponry were swarming the area. Civilians screamed as they fled the scene, and police officers futilely attempted to hold the line.

"Alright," the Doctor said as the TARDIS doors opened. "J, K, this is your stop. I'll monitor from the TARDIS and guide you to the other hotspots as soon as this one's handled."

J stepped out, his weapon at the ready. "You sure you don't want to come along, Doc? You know, lend a helping hand?"

The Doctor raised his sonic screwdriver with a grin. "Oh, I'll be helping. Just not out there. Now, go!"

K gave the Doctor a curt nod before stepping out. "Keep that containment field stable. We'll be back."

As soon as the doors closed, the Doctor spun to the console, his expression darkening. "Alright, old girl," he murmured. "Let's see what these rogue aliens are really up to."

Chaos in the Streets

J and K moved swiftly through the debris-filled streets, using their MIB weapons to neutralize the rogue aliens' attacks. A towering insectoid alien hissed as it lunged toward J, its bladed arms gleaming in the flickering streetlights.

"Ugly and mean," J muttered, firing a plasma shot that struck the alien square in the chest. It screeched and collapsed, its weapon clattering to the ground.

"Focus," K said, his weapon firing with precision at another alien attempting to flank them. "They're buying time. This isn't the main attack."

J ducked behind a fallen beam, catching his breath. "You think they're just stalling? For what?"

"That's what we're going to find out," K replied, scanning the area for any sign of a command structure.

The Doctor's Revelation

Back in the TARDIS, the Doctor worked tirelessly, scanning the energy signatures of the rogue aliens. The holographic map shifted as he pieced together their strategy. His face lit up as a new pattern emerged.

"Ah, there it is," he muttered. "They're not just distracting us—they're creating a network."

The Doctor activated his communicator. "J, K, listen carefully. The rogue aliens are setting up energy amplifiers around the city. They're forming a grid to channel power directly to the Bug. If they succeed, they'll supercharge the shard, and the rift will rip open in seconds."

"Where are these amplifiers?" K asked, his voice sharp.

The Doctor adjusted the map, highlighting three key locations: the subway system, a power plant, and the mayor's office. "Take out the amplifiers, and the grid collapses. I'll guide you to the closest one now."

The Battle for the City

The agents moved quickly, splitting their forces to tackle the amplifiers. J led a team into the subway, where the tunnels were crawling with reptilian aliens guarding a pulsating device attached to the walls.

"Alright, people," J said, raising his weapon. "We go in fast, we go in hard, and we get out before these things know what hit them."

The team charged, their weapons lighting up the dark tunnels as the aliens screeched in surprise. J fired at the amplifier, its casing sparking as it began to destabilize.

Meanwhile, K's team infiltrated the power plant, where a group of hulking, armored aliens stood guard. K moved with precision, taking down enemies one by one as his team planted explosives around the amplifier.

"Three minutes until detonation," K said into his communicator. "Make sure the next one's handled."

A Desperate Move

The Doctor monitored the progress from the TARDIS, his fingers flying over the controls. "Good work, everyone. One amplifier down, two to go. But hurry—time's running out."

Suddenly, the containment field around the Bug flickered. The Doctor froze, his eyes narrowing. "No, no, no. Stay put, you stubborn creature."

The Bug screeched, slamming against the field. Sparks flew as the shard in its chest glowed brighter, feeding off the energy grid the aliens had managed to partially activate.

"Doctor," Zed's voice crackled over the comms, "we've got more reports of alien reinforcements across the city. We're losing control out here."

The Doctor gripped the console, his expression hardening. "Then we don't give them time to regroup. K, J, finish those amplifiers. I'll keep the Bug contained as long as I can."

The Clock is Ticking

J and K fought their way through relentless waves of aliens, each team narrowly managing to disable their assigned amplifier. Explosions rocked the city as the devices went offline, and the grid began to collapse.

Back in the TARDIS, the Doctor adjusted the containment field, stabilizing it just as the Bug let out a furious roar. "Nice try," he said, sweat beading on his forehead. "But you're not winning today."

With the amplifiers destroyed and the Bug still trapped, the rogue aliens began retreating. K and J regrouped, exhausted but victorious.

"We did it," J said, slumping against a wall. "Tell me that was the last of them."

The Doctor's voice came through their earpieces, weary but triumphant. "For now. But don't get too comfortable. The Bug's still here, and her masters won't stop until they've ripped this planet apart."

K straightened, his jaw set. "Then let's make sure that doesn't happen."

As the city began to calm, the Doctor, K, and J prepared for the next stage of their battle—a confrontation that would determine the fate of Earth itself.

Chapter 18: The Battle for New York

The city was a war zone. Alien ships hovered above Manhattan, their glowing lights casting an eerie hue on the chaos below. Rogue aliens swarmed the streets, smashing through barricades and overwhelming the city's defenses. Civilians screamed as they fled in all directions, while MIB agents engaged in fierce firefights, their advanced weaponry lighting up the night.

In the heart of it all, the Doctor stood alongside Agent J in an alleyway near Times Square, the faint hum of his sonic screwdriver cutting through the distant explosions.

"J," the Doctor said, his voice calm despite the chaos, "we're running out of time. The Bug's containment field is weakening, and if I don't get back to the TARDIS, the rift will open."

J adjusted his weapon, glancing toward the skyline where the Bug's massive silhouette loomed near the energy hub. "I hear you, Doc. But getting through that mess isn't exactly a walk in the park."

The Doctor grinned, his eyes sparkling with determination. "Good thing I'm not much for walking."

K Takes Command

Meanwhile, in the MIB mobile command center, Agent K stood over a holographic map of the city, barking orders into his communicator.

"Team Alpha, hold the line at Fifth Avenue. Team Bravo, flank those ships near Central Park. Team Charlie, secure the civilians near the financial district."

Zed's voice crackled through the comms. "K, the rogue aliens are converging on the hub. If we lose that position—"

"We won't," K interrupted, his voice steady. "I've got a plan. Just keep the pressure on. And Zed—" K paused, his eyes narrowing. "Tell the Doctor he'd better deliver."

The Doctor's Plan

The Doctor and J moved through the war-torn streets, dodging alien patrols and collapsed debris. The TARDIS was their goal, its containment field barely visible in the distance.

"Alright," J said, ducking behind an overturned car as a group of insectoid aliens passed by. "Care to explain how we're supposed to fight our way through this?"

"Simple," the Doctor replied, peeking out from their cover. "We don't fight. We outthink."

J raised an eyebrow. "Yeah, because that always works."

"It does," the Doctor said, a touch of pride in his voice. "Trust me, J. The key to survival isn't brute force—it's knowing when to run."

J smirked. "Well, you're in luck, Doc. I'm great at running."

The two darted from their hiding spot, weaving through the chaos as the Doctor used his sonic screwdriver to disable alien weapons and create distractions. As they reached the edge of Times Square, they were confronted by a towering reptilian alien clad in shimmering armor.

"Ah," the Doctor said, holding up his hands. "Big, scary, and shiny. Just my luck."

The alien hissed, raising a plasma weapon. J fired first, his shot hitting the creature square in the chest. It stumbled back, roaring in pain.

"That's one way to negotiate," the Doctor muttered as they continued running.

The Massive Battle

Across the city, K led the MIB agents in an all-out assault against the rogue aliens. The skies were alive with streaks of green and blue energy as the agents' weapons clashed with the invaders' advanced technology.

"Hold the line!" K shouted, taking cover behind a barricade as a group of insectoid aliens charged. He fired several precise shots, taking down two of them before they could get close.

Nearby, an MIB vehicle transformed into a mobile turret, firing at an alien ship hovering above. The explosion lit up the night, drawing cheers from the agents below.

"K," Zed's voice came through the communicator, "we've got a swarm heading your way. ETA two minutes."

K glanced at the horizon, where a mass of glowing eyes and clawed limbs was approaching fast. "Understood," he replied. "All units, prepare for heavy contact."

Back to the TARDIS

The Doctor and J finally reached the TARDIS, its containment field flickering dangerously. The Bug was thrashing inside, her claws sparking against the glowing energy barrier.

"She's breaking free," the Doctor muttered, his voice filled with urgency. "We don't have much time."

J looked at the writhing creature, his face a mix of awe and fear. "And what's the plan if she gets out?"

The Doctor adjusted his bow tie, his eyes narrowing. "We don't let her."

He darted into the TARDIS, motioning for J to follow. Inside, the ship's interior was in chaos. Sparks flew from the central console, and the glowing columns flickered erratically.

"She's still connected to the shard," the Doctor explained as he worked the controls. "That's how she's drawing power. If I can sever the connection, the containment field will stabilize, and we can trap her permanently."

"And if you can't?" J asked, gripping his weapon tightly.

The Doctor gave him a reassuring smile. "Then I hope you're as good a shot as you say."

The Bug Escapes

Just as the Doctor began rerouting power to the containment field, a deafening screech filled the air. The Bug's claws pierced through the barrier, shattering it in a burst of energy. She lunged toward the TARDIS, her massive form squeezing through the doors.

"J, keep her busy!" the Doctor shouted, frantically adjusting the controls.

"Busy?" J yelled, firing his weapon at the creature. "How exactly am I supposed to keep that thing busy?"

The Bug snarled, swiping at J and narrowly missing him. Her glowing eyes locked onto the TARDIS console, and she began clawing her way toward it.

"She's heading for the dimensional controls!" the Doctor shouted. "If she activates them, the rift will open!"

J fired another shot, this time striking the shard embedded in the Bug's chest. The creature screeched in pain, momentarily distracted.

"Good shot!" the Doctor called out. "Keep her off the console!"

The Rift Grows

Outside, the dimensional rift began to glow brighter, its energy spilling into the sky. K and his team watched in horror as the rogue aliens rallied around it, using the chaos to intensify their assault.

"We're losing control!" an agent shouted.

"Not yet," K replied, firing at an alien ship overhead. "The Doctor's got this."

Inside the TARDIS, the Doctor activated a final sequence on the console. The room trembled as the ship's core glowed brightly, emitting a powerful pulse that sent the Bug sprawling.

"Gotcha!" the Doctor exclaimed. "Her connection's severed!"

The Bug screeched in fury, retreating toward the TARDIS doors. With a final, desperate lunge, she burst out into the city.

"She's heading for the rift!" J shouted.

The Doctor's face darkened. "Then we follow her. This ends now."

The Final Pursuit

The Doctor and J sprinted out of the TARDIS, joining K and the MIB agents in the heart of the battle. The Bug was making her final push toward the rift, her glowing shard pulsating with dangerous energy.

"K, J," the Doctor said, his voice filled with determination, "buy me some time. I'll handle the rift."

K nodded, raising his weapon. "You heard him. Let's finish this."

As the MIB launched their final assault against the rogue aliens and the Bug, the Doctor raced toward the rift, his sonic screwdriver in hand. The fate of New York—and the world—hung in the balance.

Chapter 19: The Invasion Begins

The night sky above New York City burned with an eerie, unnatural light. The dimensional rift had started to open, a swirling vortex of energy crackling with chaotic power. Alien ships, sleek and ominous, began to emerge one by one, their silhouettes casting long shadows over the chaotic city below.

At the center of it all was the Bug, perched on top of the energy hub, her massive form illuminated by the glow of the rift. The shard embedded in her chest pulsed in rhythm with the rift, acting as the anchor that tethered the gateway between dimensions.

The Doctor and J on the Move

Inside a commandeered MIB vehicle, the Doctor and J raced through the devastated streets toward the energy hub. Explosions rocked the city as rogue alien forces clashed with MIB agents, their advanced weaponry lighting up the night.

"Faster, J!" the Doctor shouted, gripping the dashboard as the car swerved to avoid a collapsing building. "We're running out of time!"

J gritted his teeth, weaving through debris and abandoned vehicles. "You think I don't know that? I've got a giant alien rift in the sky and a bug with an attitude problem on my radar!"

The Doctor leaned out of the window, his sonic screwdriver buzzing as he scanned the rift. His face darkened as he read the data. "It's worse than I thought," he muttered. "The rift isn't just a doorway—it's destabilizing the dimensional fabric. If it keeps growing, it'll pull this entire city into the void."

J glanced at him, his expression grim. "And let me guess: you've got a plan to stop it?"

The Doctor gave him a tight smile. "Oh, I've always got a plan. Just not sure if it'll work yet."

"Fantastic," J muttered, flooring the accelerator as they neared the hub.

At the Energy Hub

K and the MIB agents were already engaged in a desperate battle at the base of the energy hub. Rogue aliens swarmed the area, protecting the Bug as she continued her work on the rift. Energy beams lit up the sky as the agents fought valiantly, but the tide of the battle was shifting in favor of the invaders.

K crouched behind a barricade, firing precise shots at a group of insectoid aliens attempting to flank his position. His voice crackled through the communicator. "Zed, we need reinforcements at the hub. The Doctor's plan better work, or this city's done for."

Zed's voice came through, tense but steady. "We're deploying every available agent. Hold your position."

K glanced up at the rift, which was growing larger with each passing second. "We don't have much longer."

The Doctor and J Arrive

The MIB vehicle screeched to a halt near the barricades, and the Doctor and J jumped out, immediately taking cover as an explosion rocked the area. The Doctor's eyes locked onto the Bug, her massive form silhouetted against the swirling vortex of the rift.

"There she is," the Doctor said, his voice low. "The shard's fully activated. She's stabilizing the rift for the invasion."

J fired at a group of rogue aliens advancing toward them, his shots forcing them back. "So how do we stop her?"

The Doctor's eyes narrowed as he formulated a plan. "We need to disrupt her connection to the shard. It's the key to the rift. Sever that link, and the rift will collapse."

J reloaded his weapon, nodding. "Alright, sounds easy enough. What's the catch?"

The Doctor gave him a wry smile. "The shard's energy is interlinked with her biology. If we try to forcefully remove it, the resulting feedback could destroy half the city."

J groaned. "Of course it could. So what's the not-destroy-half-the-city option?"

The Doctor adjusted his sonic screwdriver, his mind racing. "We overload the shard with a counter-frequency, destabilize it from within. But to do that, I need to get close—dangerously close."

J stared at him. "You're seriously planning to run up to that thing while she's tearing the city apart?"

The Doctor nodded, his face set with determination. "It's the only way."

Breaking Through the Defenses

The Doctor and J pushed forward, weaving through the chaos as MIB agents covered their advance. K joined them, his expression grim but focused.

"Doctor," K said, firing at an alien attempting to flank their position, "you've got five minutes to make this work. After that, we're out of options."

"Five minutes is more than enough!" the Doctor replied, ducking as a plasma bolt whizzed past his head. "Probably."

As they reached the base of the energy hub, the Bug let out a deafening screech, her glowing eyes locking onto the group. She leaped down from her perch, landing with a thunderous crash that sent shockwaves rippling through the ground.

"J, K, keep her distracted!" the Doctor shouted, darting toward the base of the hub. "I'll handle the shard!"

"Great," J muttered, firing at the Bug as she charged toward them. "Why do we always get the fun jobs?"

The Doctor vs. the Rift

The Doctor reached the base of the hub, his sonic screwdriver buzzing as he scanned the shard's energy signature. He muttered to himself as he worked, adjusting the settings and rerouting power from the TARDIS, which was still projecting its containment field.

"Come on, come on," he murmured, his hands moving frantically. "Just need to isolate the frequency..."

Above him, the rift pulsed violently, sending waves of energy cascading down into the city. The Doctor glanced up, his face pale. "No pressure."

The Final Confrontation

Meanwhile, J and K fought valiantly to keep the Bug occupied. The creature's claws tore through barricades and vehicles as she advanced, her screeches echoing through the battlefield.

"She's not going down!" J shouted, firing another shot that glanced off her armored exoskeleton.

K's voice was calm but firm. "We're not trying to kill her. Just keep her busy."

The Bug roared, lunging toward them, but at the last moment, a blinding flash of light erupted from the base of the hub. The Doctor stood, his sonic screwdriver pointed toward the shard, which was now glowing erratically.

"Got it!" the Doctor shouted. "The shard's destabilizing!"

The Bug screeched in fury, turning toward him. J and K fired in unison, their shots striking her legs and slowing her advance.

The Rift Collapses

The rift began to pulsate wildly, its energy spiraling out of control as the shard's connection faltered. Alien ships hovering near the gateway were pulled back into the void, their engines powerless against the collapsing vortex.

"Doctor!" K shouted. "Whatever you're doing, finish it now!"

The Doctor adjusted the final setting on his screwdriver and aimed it at the shard. "Goodbye, Bug," he said softly before activating the device.

A wave of energy surged outward, engulfing the Bug and severing her connection to the shard. The rift collapsed in a spectacular explosion of light, and the remaining alien forces scattered, their invasion halted.

Aftermath

The battlefield fell silent as the dust settled. The Doctor stood near the smoldering remains of the shard, his shoulders slumped in exhaustion.

J approached, his weapon lowered. "Did we win?"

The Doctor nodded, a faint smile on his face. "We won. But only just."

K joined them, surveying the devastation around the energy hub. "What about the Bug?"

The Doctor's expression darkened. "She's gone. But her masters... they're still out there."

J sighed, shaking his head. "Of course they are. Because nothing's ever simple with you, is it, Doc?"

The Doctor chuckled softly. "Simple? Where's the fun in that?"

As the city began to recover, the Doctor, J, and K stood together, knowing that while this battle was over, the fight to protect Earth was far from finished.

Chapter 20: Facing the Bug

The air was electric with tension as the Doctor stepped into the center of the energy hub. The swirling remnants of the dimensional rift cast an eerie glow across the darkened city. At the heart of the chaos stood the Bug, her massive form towering over the machinery, the shard embedded in her chest glowing brighter with every second.

The Doctor approached cautiously, his sonic screwdriver buzzing faintly in his hand. His face was calm, but his eyes burned with determination.

The Doctor's Attempt at Diplomacy

"Hello again!" the Doctor called out, his voice echoing through the shattered structure. "We keep meeting like this, don't we? I'm starting to think you like my company."

The Bug turned her glowing, multifaceted eyes toward him, letting out a guttural screech. Her claws raked against the metal floor, sending sparks flying.

"That's not a very friendly hello," the Doctor said, raising his hands in a gesture of peace. "But I get it. You're upset. You've got this big, ambitious plan to open a rift and let your masters through. But here's the thing—it's not going to work. Not the way you think it will."

The Bug took a step closer, her massive claws digging into the floor. She screeched again, her movements twitchy and aggressive.

The Doctor sighed. "I know you've been manipulated. They planted that shard in you, turned you into their puppet. You think this is your purpose, your destiny, but it's not. You're being used, just like the rift."

The Bug lunged suddenly, swiping at him with her claws. The Doctor dodged just in time, stumbling back as her strike gouged a deep scar into the metal behind him.

"Right," he muttered, straightening his bow tie. "Not in a chatty mood, then. That's unfortunate."

The Fight Begins

The Bug roared, charging toward the Doctor. Her massive form sent shockwaves rippling through the structure as she moved. The Doctor scrambled to his feet, darting behind a collapsed console for cover.

From the TARDIS, J's voice crackled through the communicator. "Doc, what's going on in there? We're seeing some serious movement near the rift."

"Yes, well," the Doctor replied breathlessly, "I'm currently engaged in a rather one-sided conversation with our friend here. She's not a fan of constructive criticism."

J groaned. "You need backup?"

"No!" the Doctor said quickly, peeking out from behind his cover. "She's focused on me, which is exactly where I need her. Just keep the perimeter secure and make sure no one else gets hurt."

The Bug smashed through a series of support beams, her claws slicing through metal as if it were paper. Sparks flew as the structure groaned under the strain.

"Alright," the Doctor muttered, adjusting his sonic screwdriver. "Time for Plan B. Or is it Plan C? I've lost count."

Using the TARDIS

The Doctor bolted toward the TARDIS, narrowly avoiding another swipe from the Bug. He burst through the doors and immediately began working the controls, his hands moving in a blur.

"Okay, old girl," he said, his voice steady despite the chaos. "Let's show her what you can do."

The TARDIS groaned as the Doctor rerouted power to the dimensional stabilizers. On the console's screen, the remnants of the rift flickered, and the shard's energy signature spiked.

The Bug roared outside, sensing the shift in energy. She charged toward the TARDIS, her claws slamming into its blue exterior. The ship shuddered but held firm.

"Not so fast!" the Doctor called out, flipping a switch. The TARDIS emitted a powerful pulse of energy, sending the Bug staggering backward. Her screeches echoed through the structure as the shard in her chest dimmed slightly.

"That got your attention, didn't it?" the Doctor said, a hint of triumph in his voice.

The Final Confrontation

The Bug, enraged, lunged at the TARDIS again. This time, the Doctor stepped outside, sonic screwdriver in hand. The shard in her chest pulsed wildly, resonating with the remnants of the rift.

"Listen to me!" the Doctor shouted, his voice cutting through the chaos. "You don't have to do this! The shard is controlling you, forcing you to obey their will. But you can fight it. You're more than just a tool for destruction."

The Bug paused for a moment, her claws hovering inches from the Doctor. Her glowing eyes flickered, as if she were struggling against the shard's influence.

"That's it," the Doctor said softly. "You're not a puppet. You have a choice."

The shard pulsed violently, and the Bug let out a deafening screech. Her claws slammed into the ground, narrowly missing the Doctor as the rift began to expand again.

"Or maybe not," the Doctor muttered, diving out of the way.

Disrupting the Rift

The Doctor sprinted back to the TARDIS, frantically adjusting the controls. "If she won't stop, then we'll have to end this the hard way," he said to himself. He routed all of the TARDIS's power into a final, desperate maneuver.

Outside, the TARDIS emitted a high-pitched whine as its stabilizers began to disrupt the shard's connection to the rift. The Bug thrashed wildly, her screeches becoming more erratic as the shard's energy dimmed.

"Almost there," the Doctor muttered, sweat dripping down his face. "Come on, come on..."

The TARDIS emitted a blinding pulse of light, and the shard shattered in a burst of energy. The Bug let out a final, ear-splitting roar before collapsing to the ground. The rift flickered and then closed with a deafening crack, leaving the city in silence.

Aftermath

The Doctor stepped out of the TARDIS, his shoulders slumped in exhaustion. J and K approached cautiously, their weapons still at the ready.

"Is it over?" J asked, glancing at the motionless Bug.

The Doctor nodded, his face somber. "The rift is closed. The shard is gone. She won't hurt anyone anymore."

K studied the scene, his expression unreadable. "And her masters?"

The Doctor's eyes darkened. "Still out there. This was just one move in a much larger game."

J sighed, shaking his head. "Man, I hate it when you say stuff like that."

The Doctor managed a faint smile. "Cheer up, J. We saved the world. That's got to count for something."

As the sun began to rise over the city, the Doctor, J, and K stood together, knowing that while this battle was over, the fight was far from finished.

Chapter 21: The Sacrifice

The energy hub trembled violently, its foundations groaning as the remnants of the dimensional rift flickered in the air. The Bug, weakened but far from defeated, let out a guttural roar as she staggered to her feet, her glowing shard pulsing erratically. Around her, the shattered remains of MIB's defenses lay strewn across the battlefield, a grim testament to the cost of the fight.

The Doctor stood near the TARDIS, his sonic screwdriver buzzing as he frantically adjusted the ship's energy output. J crouched nearby, reloading his weapon with practiced urgency. Agent K stood ahead of them both, his weapon trained on the Bug, his face set in grim determination.

A Grim Reality

"K!" the Doctor called out, his voice tense. "We need more time to disrupt the shard's connection to the rift. If she reactivates it, we're all done for!"

K didn't look back, his eyes fixed on the Bug. "You focus on the rift, Doctor. I'll handle her."

J glanced at him, his brow furrowed with concern. "K, don't do anything crazy. We've come this far—don't go pulling a hero move now."

K's lips tightened into a faint smile. "Someone's got to keep her off you two, and I don't see anyone else volunteering."

The Doctor straightened, stepping toward him. "K, listen to me. We can figure this out together. We don't need sacrifices. That's not how I do things."

K turned to face him, his voice calm but resolute. "And that's why you need someone like me. Your plans are brilliant, Doctor, but they don't always account for the human cost. Sometimes, the only way to win is to make sure the right people survive. That's you and J."

J stood, his fists clenched. "K, come on. We're a team. You don't have to do this."

K shook his head, his gaze softening. "It's my call, kid. Always has been. Now stick to the plan and don't let it be for nothing."

The Final Stand

The Bug let out a guttural screech, her claws slamming into the ground as she lunged forward, her glowing eyes locked on the TARDIS. K stepped into her path, firing a series of precise shots that struck the shard embedded in her chest. Sparks flew as the energy within the shard crackled, momentarily forcing her back.

"Come on, you ugly thing," K muttered, reloading his weapon. "Let's dance."

The Bug roared, swiping at K with her massive claws. He dodged with practiced agility, firing another round that struck her leg and forced her to stumble. Every move he made was calculated, every shot designed to slow her down and keep her attention away from the Doctor and J.

Behind him, the Doctor worked frantically at the TARDIS console. "I'm almost there!" he shouted. "Just a few more adjustments!"

"Doctor," J said, his voice strained as he fired at a group of rogue aliens attempting to flank them, "he's not going to make it if we don't help him!"

The Doctor shook his head, his expression tight with frustration. "If we don't finish this now, no one makes it. K knows what he's doing."

The Sacrifice

The Bug let out another roar, surging forward with renewed ferocity. K fired a final shot, striking her square in the shard, but the energy rebounded, sending him sprawling to the ground. His weapon clattered out of reach as the Bug loomed over him, her claws raised for a killing blow.

"No!" J shouted, starting to run toward him.

K raised a hand, stopping him in his tracks. "Stay back, J! Don't blow this!"

The Doctor looked up from the console, his face pale. "K, get out of there!"

K met his gaze, a faint smile on his lips. "You've got this, Doctor. Save the world."

As the Bug's claws came down, K reached into his vest and activated a small device in his hand—a portable energy disruptor. A blinding flash of light erupted from the device, engulfing both him and the Bug in a wave of energy. The creature let out an earsplitting screech as the shard in her chest shattered completely, and her massive form crumpled to the ground.

The battlefield fell eerily silent.

Aftermath

J stood frozen, his weapon hanging limply at his side. "No," he whispered, his voice breaking. "No, no, no!"

The Doctor stepped out of the TARDIS, his face etched with grief. He placed a hand on J's shoulder, his voice quiet. "He knew what he was doing. He gave us a chance to finish this."

J shook his head, tears streaming down his face. "He didn't have to die! There had to be another way!"

The Doctor looked at the smoldering remains of the Bug, his eyes filled with pain. "Sometimes there isn't. Sometimes the only way to win is to lose something important. K understood that."

Zed's voice crackled through the communicator. "Doctor, J, what's the status?"

J swallowed hard, his voice trembling as he responded. "The Bug's down. The shard's destroyed. But K... he's gone."

There was a long pause before Zed's voice returned, heavy with emotion. "Understood. Get back to base. We'll honor him properly."

The Doctor's Resolve

As the Doctor and J made their way back to the TARDIS, the young agent's grief was palpable. The Doctor placed a hand on his shoulder, his voice soft but firm. "K's sacrifice won't be in vain. We've stopped the invasion, but the threat isn't over. His masters are still out there. And I promise you, J, we'll stop them. For him. For everyone."

J nodded, his jaw tightening as he wiped his tears. "Then let's get to work."

The Doctor stepped into the TARDIS, his face a mask of determination. As the doors closed behind him, the familiar hum of the ship filled the air, a reminder that the fight was far from over. But with K's memory fueling their resolve, the Doctor and J knew they would face whatever came next—together.

Chapter 22: The Rift Collapses

The TARDIS hummed with barely contained energy, its glowing console casting an unsteady light across the room. The Doctor worked frantically, his hands a blur as he adjusted levers, flipped switches, and recalibrated the TARDIS's systems. Outside, the rift pulsed violently, its swirling vortex growing wider with every passing second. The alien ships pouring through the breach cast dark shadows over the devastated city, their engines roaring as they descended.

The Doctor's Plan

J leaned against the TARDIS console, sweat streaking his face, his weapon still clutched tightly in one hand. "Doc, these ships just keep coming. Whatever you're planning, it better work."

The Doctor didn't look up, his voice clipped with urgency. "It's not about stopping them anymore, J. It's about reversing the damage. The rift is like a wound in the fabric of reality. We can't just seal it; we have to force it to collapse in on itself."

"And by 'force,'" J said, raising an eyebrow, "you mean...?"

The Doctor straightened, his eyes blazing. "We're going to use the TARDIS to reverse the polarity of the dimensional flow. Instead of pulling things into this dimension, we'll push them back into their own."

J stared at him. "You're serious?"

"Deadly serious," the Doctor replied, already darting to another console. "But it's risky. Once the rift collapses, the energy backlash could destabilize the entire area. We have to time it perfectly."

"Great," J muttered. "No pressure."

A Desperate Race

Outside, the Bug climbed to the top of the energy hub, her massive form silhouetted against the glowing rift. The remnants of the shard in her chest flickered faintly, its energy barely holding together. Yet, even weakened, her determination was palpable. She screeched, her claws slamming into the structure as she attempted to stabilize the rift herself.

"She's still trying to open it," the Doctor muttered, glancing at the TARDIS's monitor. "Even with the shard shattered, she's using her connection to the rift to keep it active. If we don't stop her, she'll succeed."

J gripped his weapon, his jaw tightening. "Then let's stop her."

"No," the Doctor said sharply, holding up a hand. "This isn't about fighting her. It's about outsmarting her. We have to cut her connection to the rift before we reverse it. Otherwise, she'll drag the entire planet into her dimension."

Confronting the Bug

The Doctor and J stepped out of the TARDIS and onto the shattered remnants of the energy hub. The ground trembled beneath them as alien ships hovered overhead, firing sporadically at MIB agents still battling on the streets below. The rift pulsed violently, its energy crackling in the air like a storm on the verge of breaking.

The Bug turned to face them, her glowing eyes burning with rage. She let out a deafening screech, her claws raking against the metal structure as she moved toward them.

"Doctor!" J shouted, aiming his weapon. "She's coming!"

"Wait!" the Doctor called out, stepping forward. He raised his sonic screwdriver, the device buzzing faintly as he pointed it toward the Bug. "Listen to me!"

The Bug paused, her massive form looming over him. Her multifaceted eyes flickered, the shard in her chest pulsing erratically.

"You don't have to do this," the Doctor said, his voice calm but firm. "I know what they did to you. They turned you into a weapon, a pawn in their game. But you're more than that. You can choose to stop."

The Bug screeched again, louder this time, and swiped at the Doctor. He ducked, the claws narrowly missing him as they gouged deep scars into the ground.

J fired a warning shot, hitting the Bug's leg and forcing her to stumble. "I don't think she's in the mood to talk, Doc!"

The Doctor scrambled back to his feet, his voice rising over the chaos. "You're fighting for them, but they'll abandon you the moment you're no longer useful. Don't let them win. Help me stop this before it's too late!"

The Bug hesitated, her movements slowing for a moment as if she were considering his words. But the shard in her chest pulsed violently, and she let out another screech, resuming her attack.

Reversing the Rift

The Doctor darted back toward the TARDIS, shouting over his shoulder. "J, keep her occupied! I need two more minutes!"

"Two minutes?" J fired at the Bug again, his shots barely slowing her advance. "She's not exactly the patient type, Doc!"

The Doctor slammed the TARDIS doors shut and raced to the console. He adjusted the controls, rerouting the ship's power to the dimensional stabilizers. The central column glowed brighter, and the hum of the engines grew louder.

"Come on, come on," the Doctor muttered, his hands moving in a blur. "Just a little more..."

Outside, J fired a final shot, hitting the shard in the Bug's chest. The creature staggered, roaring in pain, but her resolve remained unbroken. She lunged toward the TARDIS, her claws slamming into the ground just as the ship emitted a blinding pulse of energy.

The rift flickered violently, its swirling vortex beginning to reverse. Alien ships near the breach were suddenly pulled backward, their engines straining as they were dragged back into the void.

The Bug's Final Stand

The Bug screeched in fury as the rift's pull intensified. Her claws dug into the ground, anchoring her massive form as she fought against the collapsing vortex. The remnants of the shard in her chest glowed brightly, feeding off the rift's energy in a desperate attempt to stabilize it.

Inside the TARDIS, the Doctor shouted into his communicator. "J, get out of there! The rift's collapsing!"

J hesitated, glancing at the Bug. "What about her?"

The Doctor's voice softened. "She's made her choice. You can't save her now."

J nodded reluctantly and sprinted toward the TARDIS, diving inside just as the rift emitted a final, deafening roar. The Bug let out one last screech as the shard shattered completely, and she was pulled into the collapsing vortex along with the alien ships.

The rift imploded in a burst of light, leaving only silence in its wake.

Aftermath

The TARDIS interior was eerily quiet as the Doctor leaned against the console, his shoulders slumped with exhaustion. J stood nearby, his weapon still in hand, his face a mixture of relief and sorrow.

"It's over," J said quietly. "Right?"

The Doctor nodded, though his expression was somber. "For now. The rift is closed, and the invasion's been stopped. But her masters are still out there. This was just a test—a way to gauge Earth's defenses."

J shook his head, his voice heavy. "K's gone. A lot of good people are gone. And for what?"

The Doctor looked up, his eyes filled with quiet determination. "For a chance. A chance to save this planet, to protect it from what's coming. And we will, J. Together."

As the TARDIS hummed softly around them, the Doctor and J prepared to face whatever challenges lay ahead, knowing that the battle for Earth was far from over.

Chapter 23: The Final Showdown

The TARDIS interior hummed with strained energy as the Doctor stood at the console, his hands flying over the controls. The collapsing dimensional rift had left the city battered, but the immediate danger seemed to have passed. Yet, in the back of his mind, the Doctor couldn't shake the nagging feeling that something was unfinished.

"Doc," J said, leaning heavily against a railing, his weapon still in hand. His voice was steady, but exhaustion crept into its edges. "We've got the rift closed, the ships are gone, and the city's not a smoking crater. What's left?"

The Doctor didn't look up from the console, his face tense with concentration. "The Bug. She's not gone, J. Not yet."

J's expression hardened. "Come on, Doc. The rift pulled her in. She's history."

The Doctor shook his head, the TARDIS's monitors reflecting in his determined eyes. "No. She's still here. I can feel her presence in the TARDIS systems. She's trying to hijack the ship."

Suddenly, the TARDIS shook violently, sending J stumbling. The central column pulsed erratically, the light inside flickering like a heartbeat under strain.

"Yep," J said, gripping the railing tightly. "That's not good."

The Doctor spun around, his voice sharp. "Not good? That's catastrophic! She's inside the TARDIS, using the ship's temporal engines to escape. If she gains control, she could open another rift—anywhere, anytime. And this time, we might not be able to stop her."

The Bug Revealed

The TARDIS groaned again, and a screech echoed through the ship, reverberating off the walls. The Doctor's face darkened. "She's in the engine room."

J raised his weapon. "Then let's finish this."

The Doctor held up a hand, stopping him. "No weapons, J. This is the TARDIS—she's alive, and she won't take kindly to stray shots. Besides, I have a better idea."

J frowned but nodded. "Alright, Doc. Lead the way."

The Doctor grabbed his sonic screwdriver and darted toward the corridors, with J close behind. The lights flickered ominously as the ship trembled under the strain of the Bug's interference.

They reached the engine room, a vast chamber filled with glowing orbs and streams of temporal energy flowing like rivers of light. At the center of it all was the Bug, her massive form illuminated by the pulsing engines. The shard in her chest was gone, but her connection to the TARDIS's power was undeniable. Tendrils of temporal energy snaked around her, feeding her strength.

"You're persistent, I'll give you that," the Doctor called out, stepping forward. His voice was calm, but his eyes burned with determination. "But you've made one very big mistake."

The Bug turned her glowing eyes toward him, letting out a guttural screech that shook the room.

J winced, raising his weapon instinctively. "What mistake?"

The Doctor smirked. "She picked the wrong ship to mess with."

The Temporal Trap

The Bug lunged toward the Doctor, her claws swiping through the air. The Doctor rolled out of the way, narrowly avoiding her attack. He scrambled to his feet, his sonic screwdriver buzzing as he scanned the room.

"J, keep her attention!" the Doctor shouted, darting toward a console embedded in the wall.

"Keep her attention?" J fired a warning shot at the ground near the Bug, drawing her gaze. "Sure, why not? Hey, ugly! Over here!"

The Bug roared, turning her massive form toward J. She lunged again, her claws raking against the floor as J dove behind a pillar.

Meanwhile, the Doctor worked quickly, his hands moving in a blur as he adjusted the TARDIS's systems. "Alright, old girl," he muttered. "Let's show her what you're made of."

The glowing streams of temporal energy began to shift, converging around the Bug. She thrashed against the currents, screeching in fury as the streams formed a glowing bubble around her.

J peeked out from behind the pillar, his eyes widening. "Doc, what's happening?"

"I'm creating a temporal bubble," the Doctor said, his voice rising with excitement. "It's a pocket of frozen time, separate from the rest of the universe. Once she's inside, she won't be able to escape."

The Bug roared louder, her movements becoming more frantic as she realized what was happening. The temporal energy tightened around her, glowing brighter with every second.

"Come on," the Doctor muttered, his eyes locked on the console. "Just a little more..."

The Final Push

The Bug made one last desperate lunge toward the Doctor, her claws slashing through the air. J fired another shot, hitting the floor in front of her and forcing her back.

"Stay down, you oversized cockroach!" J shouted.

The temporal bubble glowed brightly, the energy streams locking into place around the Bug. She let out a final, earsplitting screech as the bubble sealed completely, freezing her massive form in mid-motion.

The room fell silent.

The Doctor stepped back from the console, breathing heavily. "That's it. She's trapped. Frozen in time forever."

J lowered his weapon, staring at the glowing bubble. "She can't get out?"

The Doctor shook his head. "Not unless someone tampered with the TARDIS's systems, and I've made sure that won't happen. She's a permanent fixture now, locked away where she can't hurt anyone."

J let out a long breath, slumping against a nearby railing. "Good. Because I've had just about enough of her."

Aftermath

Back in the console room, the TARDIS hummed softly, her systems returning to normal. The Doctor leaned against the console, his hands running over the familiar controls as he spoke.

"The rift is closed, the Bug is neutralized, and Earth is safe," he said. "For now."

J sat on the stairs leading to the console, his expression thoughtful. "So that's it? We're done?"

The Doctor looked at him, his face serious but kind. "For now, yes. But there will always be more threats, more dangers. Earth has a knack for attracting trouble."

J nodded slowly. "And you'll be there to stop it?"

The Doctor smiled faintly. "Always."

The TARDIS's central column began to glow steadily, its rhythmic hum filling the room with a sense of calm. The Doctor adjusted a lever, and the ship shifted slightly as it prepared to dematerialize.

"Where to next, Doc?" J asked, standing and adjusting his jacket.

The Doctor grinned, his eyes sparkling with the promise of adventure. "Anywhere and everywhere. The universe is big, J, and there's always something new to see."

As the TARDIS disappeared into the timestream, the Doctor and J left behind the chaos of the battle, ready to face whatever challenges lay ahead. Earth was safe, and for now, that was enough.

Chapter 24: Farewell to the MIB

The dawn light spread across the battered cityscape, illuminating the remnants of the battle. Smoke rose from the energy hub, and alien debris was scattered across the streets. The chaos had finally subsided, leaving behind an uneasy quiet.

The TARDIS stood at the heart of it all, its familiar blue exterior a stark contrast to the destruction around it. Inside, the Doctor worked at the console, his movements slower than usual. The adrenaline of the battle had worn off, replaced by the weight of what had been lost.

The door creaked open, and J stepped inside, his footsteps heavy. His suit was scuffed, and his tie hung loosely around his neck. In his hand, he carried K's signature weapon.

"Hey, Doc," J said, his voice quieter than usual. "They're waiting for you outside."

The Doctor looked up, offering a faint smile. "And you? How are you holding up?"

J shrugged, but his eyes betrayed his exhaustion. "I'm still here. That's something, right?"

The Doctor crossed the room, leaning against the railing near the stairs. "It is. More than something. K would be proud."

J glanced down at the weapon in his hand, his grip tightening. "Yeah, well... K always said someone had to hold the line. Guess it's my turn now."

A Somber Gathering

Outside the TARDIS, the remaining MIB agents had gathered near the wreckage of the energy hub. Zed stood at the center, his usual stern demeanor softened by the loss of his oldest agent.

As the Doctor and J stepped out, the group turned to face them. There was an unspoken reverence in the air, a collective acknowledgment of the sacrifices that had been made.

Zed cleared his throat, addressing the crowd. "We've faced threats before. We've fought battles, saved lives, and protected this planet in ways the world will never know. But today, we lost one of our own. Agent K gave his life to ensure Earth's survival. He was more than an agent—he was a leader, a friend, and a damn good man."

The agents bowed their heads, a moment of silence settling over the group.

The Doctor stepped forward, his hands clasped in front of him. "I didn't know K as long as you did, but I saw the kind of person he was. Brave, selfless, determined to do what was right no matter the cost. People like that... they're rare. And they leave a mark that doesn't fade."

J stepped up beside the Doctor, his voice steady despite the emotion in his eyes. "K taught me everything I know about this job. He always said it wasn't about the glory or the gadgets—it was about protecting people. Keeping the world safe, even when it didn't know it needed saving." He paused, taking a deep breath. "He'd want us to keep going. To keep fighting, no matter what."

Zed nodded. "And we will."

J's Promotion

As the group began to disperse, Zed pulled J aside. The Doctor watched from a distance, leaning against the TARDIS with his arms crossed.

"J," Zed said, his tone serious, "K made it clear before the mission that if anything happened to him, you were the one he trusted to step up. You're ready for this."

J blinked, caught off guard. "You're saying...?"

"You're the new K," Zed said, placing a hand on J's shoulder. "You've earned it."

J hesitated, glancing at the weapon in his hand. "I'm not sure I can fill his shoes."

"You're not supposed to," Zed said firmly. "You're supposed to be you. That's what he saw in you."

J nodded slowly, his jaw tightening. "Alright. Let's do this."

The Farewell

The Doctor approached J as he stood near the energy hub, gazing out at the recovering city.

"Well," the Doctor said softly, "I suppose this is goodbye."

J turned, a faint smile tugging at his lips. "You're just gonna disappear in that blue box of yours, aren't you?"

The Doctor chuckled. "That's usually how it goes."

J extended his hand, and the Doctor shook it firmly. "Thanks, Doc. For everything. I don't think we'd have made it without you."

The Doctor's smile faded slightly, his eyes filled with quiet resolve. "You would have. You always do. The MIB has been defending this planet long before I showed up. K was proof of that."

J looked down, his grip on K's weapon tightening. "He would've liked you. You two had the same kind of... never-quit thing going on."

The Doctor tilted his head. "I think he would've driven me mad. Too practical."

J laughed, the sound bittersweet. "Yeah, he was good at that."

The Doctor stepped back toward the TARDIS, his hands sliding into his coat pockets. "Take care of this planet, J. It's more special than it knows."

J nodded. "You too, Doc. Don't be a stranger."

The Doctor paused at the door, his expression softening. "You never know. The universe has a funny way of bringing people back together."

With that, he stepped inside the TARDIS. The familiar wheezing groan filled the air as the ship dematerialized, leaving J standing alone in the quiet aftermath.

A New Beginning

As the TARDIS disappeared, J turned back to the city, his new role as K weighing heavily on his shoulders. But as he looked at the recovering skyline, a spark of determination lit in his eyes.

"We've got this," he murmured to himself. "For K."

With that, he turned and walked back to the command center, ready to lead the next generation of the MIB into whatever challenges lay ahead.

Chapter 25: Onward to New Adventures

The TARDIS materialized in a quiet alley on the outskirts of Manhattan. The Doctor leaned against the console, staring at the screen that displayed the recovering city. From the fragmented skyline, he could see the remnants of the battle—the scorched buildings, the alien wreckage, and the slowly returning lights of New York City.

"Well," he said to himself, "another planet saved. Another day in the life of a madman in a box."

But his voice lacked its usual buoyant energy. This adventure had taken more out of him than he liked to admit. The weight of K's sacrifice, the devastation left behind, and the knowledge that the Bug's masters were still out there lingered in his mind.

The Doctor flipped a switch on the console, dimming the display. He turned and leaned heavily on the console, his eyes scanning the room as if looking for an answer. The hum of the TARDIS filled the silence, a constant, comforting reminder that he wasn't truly alone.

A Final Look at New York

The Doctor stepped outside the TARDIS one last time, his long coat swirling around his legs as the wind caught it. The street was eerily quiet, a stark contrast to the chaos that had engulfed the city hours earlier. The sun was rising now, casting warm hues over the broken skyline.

He took a deep breath, letting the crisp morning air fill his lungs. "You did well, New York," he murmured. "You always do."

In the distance, he spotted a group of MIB agents working to clear debris. Among them was J—or rather, the new K—giving orders with a newfound sense of authority. He watched for a moment, a faint smile tugging at his lips.

"Good hands," the Doctor said softly. "Earth's in good hands."

The Doctor Reflects

As he stepped back into the TARDIS, the Doctor's expression grew thoughtful. He ran his hand over the console, his fingers brushing the levers and dials as if they were old friends.

"K," he said aloud, his voice echoing in the cavernous interior. "You reminded me of something important. Sacrifice isn't about the loss—it's about what you leave behind. What you protect. And you've left behind a world that's better for having known you."

The TARDIS hummed gently, as if agreeing with him. The Doctor chuckled softly, shaking his head. "You always know what to say, don't you?"

He moved to the central console, adjusting the settings and pulling up the star map. The swirling vortex of time and space spun across the screen, a limitless sea of possibilities.

Choosing the Next Adventure

The Doctor stared at the map, his mind racing through potential destinations. The bright constellations, flickering stars, and unexplored regions of the universe called to him like an old song.

"Where to next, old girl?" he mused, spinning a dial and watching the stars shift on the screen. "The Andromeda Cascades? A quick hop to the Medusa Nebula? Or maybe..." His voice trailed off as a mischievous grin spread across his face. "A little trip to the Dawn Cities of Alpha Prime. I hear their sunrises are quite literally breathtaking."

The TARDIS groaned in response, the lights flickering playfully. The Doctor laughed, tapping the console affectionately. "Alright, alright, I get it. You've got your own ideas."

He adjusted a few more settings, the ship's central column beginning to pulse rhythmically. The familiar wheezing groan of the TARDIS engines filled the room as the ship prepared to dematerialize.

A Quiet Moment

Before pulling the final lever, the Doctor paused. He glanced at the photograph pinned to the edge of the console—a snapshot from another adventure, another time. His hand hovered over it for a moment, and he smiled faintly.

"Another world saved," he said softly, as if speaking to the faces in the photo. "Another chapter closed. But the story's not over yet."

With a deep breath, he pulled the lever.

Onward to New Adventures

The TARDIS shuddered as it vanished from the alley, leaving behind only the faint echo of its departure. Inside, the Doctor grinned as the ship soared through the timestream, its walls glowing with the energy of the journey.

"Onward!" he declared, his voice ringing with renewed determination. "To new adventures, new friends, and maybe—just maybe—a little bit of peace along the way."

The TARDIS surged forward, hurtling toward its next destination. Somewhere out there, in the vast expanse of time and space, another story was waiting to be written. And the Doctor, as always, was ready.

<u>Message from the Author:</u>

I hope you enjoyed this book, I love astrology and knew there was not a book such as this out on the shelf. I love metaphysical items as well. Please check out my other books:

-Life of Government Benefits

-My life of Hell

-My life with Hydrocephalus

-Red Sky

-World Domination:Woman's rule

-World Domination:Woman's Rule 2: The War

-Life and Banishment of Apophis: book 1

-The Kidney Friendly Diet

-The Ultimate Hemp Cookbook

-Creating a Dispensary(legally)

-Cleanliness throughout life: the importance of showering from childhood to adulthood.

-Strong Roots: The Risks of Overcoddling children

-Hemp Horoscopes: Cosmic Insights and Earthly Healing

- Celestial Hemp Navigating the Zodiac: Through the Green Cosmos

-Astrological Hemp: Aligning The Stars with Earth's Ancient Herb

-The Astrological Guide to Hemp: Stars, Signs, and Sacred Leaves

-Green Growth: Innovative Marketing Strategies for your Hemp Products and Dispensary

-Cosmic Cannabis

-Astrological Munchies

-Henry The Hemp

-Zodiacal Roots: The Astrological Soul Of Hemp

- **Green Constellations: Intersection of Hemp and Zodiac**

-Hemp in The Houses: An astrological Adventure Through The Cannabis Galaxy

-Galactic Ganja Guide

Heavenly Hemp

Zodiac Leaves

Doctor Who Astrology

Cannastrology

Stellar Satvias and Cosmic Indicas

Celestial Cannabis: A Zodiac Journey

AstroHerbology: The Sky and The Soil: Volume 1

AstroHerbology:Celestial Cannabis:Volume 2

Cosmic Cannabis Cultivation

The Starry Guide to Herbal Harmony: Volume 1

The Starry Guide to Herbal Harmony: Cannabis Universe: Volume 2

Yugioh Astrology: Astrological Guide to Deck, Duels and more

Nightmare Mansion: Echoes of The Abyss

Nightmare Mansion 2: Legacy of Shadows

Nightmare Mansion 3: Shadows of the Forgotten

Nightmare Mansion 4: Echoes of the Damned

The Life and Banishment of Apophis: Book 2

Nightmare Mansion: Halls of Despair

Healing with Herb: Cannabis and Hydrocephalus

Planetary Pot: Aligning with Astrological Herbs: Volume 1

Fast Track to Freedom: 30 Days to Financial Independence Using AI, Assets, and Agile Hustles

Cosmic Hemp Pathways

How to Become Financially Free in 30 Days: 10,000 Paths to Prosperity

Zodiacal Herbage: Astrological Insights: Volume 1

Nightmare Mansion: Whispers in the Walls

The Daleks Invade Atlantis

Henry the hemp and Hydrocephalus

10X The Kidney Friendly Diet

Cannabis Universe: Adult coloring book

Hemp Astrology: The Healing Power of the Stars

Zodiacal Herbage: Astrological Insights: Cannabis Universe: Volume 2

Planetary Pot: Aligning with Astrological Herbs: Cannabis Universes: Volume 2

Doctor Who Meets the Replicators and SG-1: The Ultimate Battle for Survival

Nightmare Mansion: Curse of the Blood Moon

The Celestial Stoner: A Guide to the Zodiac

Cosmic Pleasures: Sex Toy Astrology for Every Sign

Hydrocephalus Astrology: Navigating the Stars and Healing Waters

Lapis and the Mischievous Chocolate Bar

Celestial Positions: Sexual Astrology for Every Sign

Apophis's Shadow Work Journal: : A Journey of Self-Discovery and Healing

Kinky Cosmos: Sexual Kink Astrology for Every Sign

Digital Cosmos: The Astrological Digimon Compendium

Stellar Seeds: The Cosmic Guide to Growing with Astrology

Apophis's Daily Gratitude Journal

Cat Astrology: Feline Mysteries of the Cosmos

The Cosmic Kama Sutra: An Astrological Guide to Sexual Positions

Unleash Your Potential: A Guided Journal Powered by AI Insights

Whispers of the Enchanted Grove

Cosmic Pleasures: An Astrological Guide to Sexual Kinks

369, 12 Manifestation Journal

Whisper of the nocturne journal(blank journal for writing or drawing)

The Boogey Book

Locked In Reflection: A Chastity Journey Through Locktober

Generating Wealth Quickly:

How to Generate $100,000 in 24 Hours

Star Magic: Harness the Power of the Universe

The Flatulence Chronicles: A Fart Journal for Self-Discovery

The Doctor and The Death Moth

Seize the Day: A Personal Seizure Tracking Journal

The Ultimate Boogeyman Safari: A Journey into the Boogie World and Beyond

Whispers of Samhain: 1,000 Spells of Love, Luck, and Lunar Magic: Samhain Spell Book

Apophis's guides:

Witch's Spellbook Crafting Guide for Halloween

<u>Frost & Flame: The Enchanted Yule Grimoire of 1000 Winter Spells</u>

<u>The Ultimate Boogey Goo Guide & Spooky Activities for Halloween Fun</u>

Harmony of the Scales: A Libra's Spellcraft for Balance and Beauty

The Enchanted Advent: 36 Days of Christmas Wonders

Nightmare Mansion: The Labyrinth of Screams

Harvest of Enchantment: 1,000 Spells of Gratitude, Love, and Fortune for Thanksgiving

The Boogey Chronicles: A Journal of Nightly Encounters and Shadowy Secrets

The 12 Days of Financial Freedom: A Step-by-Step Christmas Countdown to Transform Your Finances

Sigil of the Eternal Spiral Blank Journal

A Christmas Feast: Timeless Recipes for Every Meal

Holiday Stress-Free Solutions: A Survival Guide to Thriving During the Festive Season

Yu-Gi-Oh! Holiday Gifting Mastery: The Ultimate Guide for Fans and Newcomers Alike

Holiday Harmony: A Hydrocephalus Survival Guide for the Festive Season

Celestial Craft: The Witch's Almanac for 2025 – A Cosmic Guide to Manifestations, Moons, and Mystical Events

Doctor Who: The Toymaker's Winter Wonderland

Tulsa King Unveiled: A Thrilling Guide to Stallone's Mafia Masterpiece

Pendulum Craft: A Complete Guide to Crafting and Using Personalized Divination Tools

Nightmare Mansion: Santa's Eternal Eve

Starlight Noel: A Cosmic Journey through Christmas Mysteries

The Dark Architect: Unlocking the Blueprint of Existence

Surviving the Embrace: The Ultimate Guide to Encounters with The Hugging Molly

The Enchanted Codex: Secrets of the Craft for Witches, Wiccans, and Pagans

Harvest of Gratitude: A Complete Thanksgiving Guide

Yuletide Essentials: A Complete Guide to an Authentic and Magical Christmas

Celestial Smokes: A Cosmic Guide to Cigars and Astrology

Living in Balance: A Comprehensive Survival Guide to Thriving with Diabetes Insipidus

Cosmic Symbiosis: The Venom Zodiac Chronicles

The Cursed Paw of Ambition

Cosmic Symbiosis: The Astrological Venom Journal

Celestial Wonders Unfold: A Stargazer's Guide to the Cosmos (2024-2029)

The Ultimate Black Friday Prepper's Guide: Mastering Shopping Strategies and Savings

Cosmic Sales: The Astrological Guide to Black Friday Shopping

Legends of the Corn Mother and Other Harvest Myths

Whispers of the Harvest: The Corn Mother's Journal

The Evergreen Spellbook

The Doctor Meets the Boogeyman

The White Witch of Rose Hall's SpellBook

The Gingerbread Golem's Shadow: A Study in Sweet Darkness

The Gingerbread Golem Codex: An Academic Exploration of Sweet Myths

The Gingerbread Golem Grimoire: Sweet Magicks and Spells for the Festive Witch

The Curse of the Gingerbread Golem

10-minute Christmas Crafts for kids

<u>Christmas Crisis Solutions: The Ultimate Last-Minute Survival Guide</u>

Gingerbread Golem Recipes: Holiday Treats with a Magical Twist

The Infinite Key: Unlocking Mystical Secrets of the Ages

Enchanted Yule: A Wiccan and Pagan Guide to a Magical and Memorable Season

Dinosaurs of Power: Unlocking Ancient Magick

Astro-Dinos: The Cosmic Guide to Prehistoric Wisdom

Gallifrey's Yule Logs: A Festive Doctor Who Cookbook

The Dino Grimoire: Secrets of Prehistoric Magick

The Gift They Never Knew They Needed

The Gingerbread Golem's Culinary Alchemy: Enchanting Recipes for a Sweetly Dark Feast

A Time Lord Christmas: Holiday Adventures with the Doctor

Krampusproofing Your Home: Defensive Strategies for Yule

Silent Frights: A Collection of Christmas Creepypastas to Chill Your Bones

Santa Raptor's Jolly Carnage: A Dino-Claus Christmas Tale

Prehistoric Palettes: A Dino Wicca Coloring Journey

The Christmas Wishkeeper Chronicles

The Starlight Sleigh: A Holiday Journey

Elf Secrets: The True Magic of the North Pole

Candy Cane Conjurations
Cooking with Kids: Recipes Under 20 Minutes

Get Some Tarot cards: https://www.makeplayingcards.com/sell/apophis-occult-shop

Get some shirts: https://www.bonfire.com/store/apophis-shirt-emporium/

<u>Instagrams:</u>
@apophis_enterprises,
@apophisbookemporium,
@apophisscardshop
Twitter: @apophisenterpr1
 Tiktok:@apophisenterprise
Youtube: @sg1fan23477, @FiresideRetreatKingdom
Hive: @sg1fan23477
CheeLee: @SG1fan23477

Podcast: Apophis Chat Zone: https://open.spotify.com/show/5zXbrCLEV2xzCp8ybrfHsk?si=fb4d4fdbdce44dec

Newsletter: https://apophiss-newsletter-27c897.beehiiv.com/

If you want to support me or see posts of other projects that I have come over to: **buymeacoffee.com/mpetchinskg**
I post there daily several times a day

Get your Dinowicca or Christmas themed digital products, especially Santa Raptor songs and other musics. Here: **https://sg1fan23477.gumroad.com**

Apophis Yuletide Digital has not only digital Christmas items, but it will have all things with Dinowicca as well as other Digital products.